Nothing Is Little

Nothing
Is Little

Carmella Van Vleet

HOLIDAY HOUSE ● NEW YORK

HOLIDAY HOUSE is registered in the U.S. Patent and Trademark Office.

Printed and bound in May 2022 at Maple Press, York, PA, USA.

www.holidayhouse.com

First Edition

1 3 5 7 9 10 8 6 4 2

Library of Congress Cataloging-in-Publication Data

Names: Van Vleet, Carmella, author.

Title: Nothing is little / by Carmella Van Vleet.

Description: First edition. | New York : Holiday House, 2022. | Includes author's
note about growth disorders. | Audience: Ages 8-12. | Audience: Grades 4-6.
Summary: "Felix, an eleven-year-old boy with Growth Hormone Deficiency
and love for forensic science, finds out his biological father is also short and
decides to find him"—Provided by publisher.

Identifiers: LCCN 2021038059 | ISBN 9780823450114 (hardcover)

Subjects: CYAC: Growth disorders—Fiction. | Forensic sciences—Fiction.
Babies—Fiction. | Fathers—Fiction. | LCGFT: Novels.

Classification: LCC PZ7.V378 No 2022 | DDC [Fic]—dc23

LC record available at https://lccn.loc.gov/2021038059

This one is for Andrea

1

THE ALIEN

Things started changing when the alien took over.

For example, Mom used to stock up on desserts during back-to-school sales. But it's two weeks into the year, and there's still nothing sweet to pack in my lunch.

"Sorry, Felix," Mom says, standing in front of the open pantry. "No Oreos."

"I put them on the grocery list," I say.

She gives me a tired smile. "I forgot to take the list."

I feel bad about complaining. Remembering stuff is hard for Mom lately. So are mornings.

We're running later than usual. Mom's in her pajamas and hasn't showered yet. She overslept on account of she's pregnant and spent the whole night getting up to pee.

For the record, my mom's not the alien. My sister is. Boo's not even born yet, and she's already causing trouble.

It's must be super weird to have some invisible being kick your bladder. The other night, Boo had the hiccups and I could actually see my mom's stomach jump every few seconds.

It's not just Mom's body. Boo has taken over our house, too. There's a bunch of baby things and boxes of diapers piling up in the dining room. And even though my sister won't be here for three more months, there's a bottle sterilizer hogging space on the kitchen counter. Mom pushes it aside to check the fruit bowl.

"We've got bananas," Mom tells me. "Or...Well, we have brown bananas."

"It's okay," I tell her. "I'll buy something at school again."

There's just enough time for me to finish up my Spanish homework, so I shove my lunch bag into my backpack and sit down.

Paul strolls into the kitchen. When he sees me he says, "A good sleep I trust you had, Padawan." He's been saying that ever since the two of us did a *Star Wars* movie marathon a few months back. I give him a thumbs-up and go back to my worksheet.

Paul walks over to Mom and rubs her middle. "How are my favorite girls this morning?" Lately, his "favorite girls" are his favorite topic. Boo has invaded Paul's vocabulary, too. He must have a Pregnancy Word of the Day calendar or something. He drops words like *gestation period, amniotic fluid,* and *placenta* (gross, gross, *aaaannd* gross) into conversations.

Mom tells Paul his favorite girls are fine, and he gives her stomach one last pat before grabbing himself coffee.

"Got a busy day?" Paul asks Mom.

She tells him she's got a focus group coming in later at her downtown office. Mom works for a market research company that gets people's opinions about different kinds of products.

"Have fun," Paul says to Mom before kissing her on the cheek.

"You too," she says as he heads to work. "Don't break anything!"

Paul is the Give It a Try Guy! on Channel 9 (*Columbus, Ohio's #1 Home for News,* according to their commercials). His job is to try out other people's jobs. He's only broken something once—when he tried being a window washer. And the window was technically only *cracked.*

After Paul is gone, Mom turns to me. "Felix. Don't forget, I'll be picking you up during fifth period for your appointment at Dr. Ryan's."

"Okay. Gotta go," I say. "Bus." I grab my backpack and fly to the front door.

"I'll go to the store after work. Want anything special?" Mom calls.

"Cookies!" I call back.

Ray is in our usual seat. I give him a quick up-nod and he does the same. We don't have any classes together and don't share the same lunch period, so the only time we can hang out is on the bus.

"You missed a hole," I say after I kick my backpack under the bench seat.

"Huh?"

I point to the top of his shirt, where he put the top button in the second hole.

"Oh. Thanks," he says. He undoes all the buttons and leaves his shirt open since he's wearing a blue T-shirt under it anyway. "There. Fixed it."

"I'm proud," I tell him all serious-like.

Ray looks over and grins because it's our inside joke. He and I stood next to each other at the Wax Museum last year.

That's this thing where the fifth graders research and dress up as famous people and then hang out in the gym, telling parents and kids in the lower grades stuff about the person.

I was Ben Franklin. And the principal came by and told me I had to stop telling people Franklin wrote an essay called "Fart Proudly." After he walked away, Ray said, "Hey, Felix. I'm proud," and then made a fart sound using his arm. The two of us spent the morning cracking each other up saying, "Hey, Ray. I'm proud," and "Hey, Felix. I'm proud," when no one was around.

Ray throws himself back against the seat. "Man, last night—" he starts, but then he's interrupted by the girl in front of us. Her name is Casey and she's wearing a shirt with shamrocks on it even though St. Patrick's Day is six months away. She's turned around and kneeling on her seat.

"Guess what?" she says.

Ray sighs. "What?" he asks. I wait. I know Casey is going to tell us. She's like a balloon that's got too much air.

"It's brilliant!" Casey says. She holds up her phone (even though we're not supposed to have them out on the bus). "I got a puppy over the weekend. Her name is Pepper. Which is short for Peppercorn. Because she's black. Wanna see?"

Despite the fact that neither of us replies, Casey shows me and Ray the picture. She's excited, and I don't want to hurt her feelings. "Cute dog," I tell her.

I asked for a puppy after Mom and Paul got married. I'm getting a sister instead.

The bus driver looks in the mirror and scolds Casey for not sitting the right way. She turns around and slides back down in her seat.

Ray shakes his head. "What was I talking about?"

"Last night," I say.

"Oh, yeah. Man. Last night my dad was being super annoying," Ray says. "He was on the Math Club thing again."

Ray's dad is an accountant and runs a big firm called Holton and Brooks. (Ray's dad is the Holton part.) Ray's dad calls it his legacy and expects Ray to become an accountant, too, and run the company someday. But Ray is into drawing and wants to become a video game artist.

"You know what he told me?" Ray goes on. "He told me he wanted to come to school and be a guest speaker."

"Did you tell him you don't want to join Math Club?"

"About a million times by now," Ray says. "You have no idea how lucky you are."

Ray has said something like this before. He means I'm lucky not to have a dad who talks about legacies and being "a chipped key off the old calculator." I've heard Ray's dad talk about accounting before. It's nerdy, but it's also cool that he wants it to be a father-son thing. I have no idea what I want to do when I get older. Paul encourages me to become whatever I want. He likes to say, *"Who am I to question someone's job? I get paid to be goofy on television."*

Paul is my stepdad.

I don't know my dad. And I don't know a single thing about him other than that he and Mom went to the same college. I asked a lot of questions when I was younger, but I got the same response from Mom: "I'll tell you about him someday. Not today." In third grade there was this father-kid thing at school and I asked about my dad again. I got the usual response, but Mom also started crying. I haven't asked since.

But I wish I knew more about him.

2

"AND DAD?"

Ten minutes before the end of fifth period, I get called down to leave for my appointment. I meet Mom in the front office. She and Ms. Markson, the school secretary, are chatting.

"How are you feeling these days?" Ms. Markson asks Mom.

"Huge," Mom says while she rubs her belly. They laugh.

"Ooo! She must know we're talking about her," Mom says.

Ms. Markson squeals and comes around from her desk. "She's kicking? Can I feel?"

Mom nods and Ms. Markson puts both of her hands right on Mom's stomach. Pretty soon both of the school counselors come out of their offices and put their hands on Mom's stomach, too. And then the principal, Ms. Good (who, for the record, likes to joke that she and I are "name cousins" because my last name is Fine), joins them. It's embarrassing enough that my mom is pregnant so, obviously, that means she, *you know,* but does she have to let everyone in the world touch her? And does she have to let them do that while I'm standing right here?

I back up closer to the door, hoping Mom gets the hint that I'm ready to go.

"Felix," Mom says, holding out her hand in my direction. "You're missing it. Come feel."

"I'm okay," I tell her.

Mom eventually pulls away and waves to her baby bump admirers, and the two of us head to the car. Even though I'm eleven, I crawl into the backseat. "It's the law," Mom likes to say. At least she bought me a less-obvious booster seat a few months ago.

"There's a bag of pretzels in the seat pocket," Mom tells me. Good. My stomach is growling.

"Thanks," I say. "I'll be sure to give you five stars in my review."

Mom and I like to joke that she's a car service since I sit in the back, like a paying customer. Last week, we pretended I was a famous actor. Mom kept calling me sir and I kept saying, "No photographs, please."

I like being short. It's my thing. People at school know me as the short kid. I've been called plenty of other things, too. Like the Elf on the Shelf, Runt, Shrimp, Keebler (as in the cookie elf). That last one is my favorite. Being called names doesn't bother me, but I have to admit that sitting in the front seat will be one good thing about getting the growth hormone shots.

Mom and I are a few minutes late to my appointment, but they're not ready for us. "I'll be right back," Mom says even before we sit down.

She has to pee. She *always* has to pee. The waiting room has an aquarium in the corner. I bet that's what did it.

Dr. Ryan's waiting room is nice. Besides the fish tank, there's a section for younger kids with toys and a table for older kids with jigsaw puzzles and tablets. It also has a mini-fridge with mini-cans of juice and a basket of snacks, since kids with juvenile diabetes also see him. (Mom says the juice and snacks are in case someone has low blood sugar.) But I'm sick of waiting rooms. In the last six months, I've become an expert on them.

It started with Dr. Kollar, my pediatrician. Mom made us go see her because she'd been reading tons of child development books because of Boo, and she started worrying that I hadn't had a growth spurt yet. Dr. Kollar said I was probably a late bloomer but sent us to Dr. Ryan as a precaution. Mom explained to me that Dr. Ryan was an endocrinologist. "That's a doctor who specializes in glands and hormones," she said.

Okay. Hormones, those I understood. We'd had the "body talk" in fifth grade. I figured an endocrinologist was a doctor you saw for puberty. But from there, I was sent to other places to get tests done, and a few months later, we went back to see Dr. Ryan. That's when he told me that the reason I'm so short is because I have growth hormone deficiency. My pituitary gland doesn't make enough growth hormone to make me grow the way I'm supposed to.

Mom bawled so hard that Dr. Ryan had to get her a handful of tissues. It was embarrassing. It also freaked me out. I thought maybe I was dying the way Mom was carrying on. (Later on, Paul told me it was pregnancy hormones that made Mom get emotional.) Mom came into my room that night and said everything would be okay, and wasn't it nice we finally knew what was going on, and it was something we could treat?

I didn't think so. Especially since I had to start getting growth hormone shots. Dr. Ryan explained that he couldn't give me a pill; growth hormones don't work that way. Mom or Paul would have to give me a shot every night until my growth plates closed, or when I stopped growing.

That's right. Shots. Every night.

I tried to argue my way out of them, but Mom was ready.

Me: What if I'm supposed to be short? Somebody has to be at the bottom of the growth charts.

Mom: Your body is missing something. It isn't producing growth hormones.

Me: I feel fine. I like being short.

Mom: It could affect other things, like your heart and bones.

Me: What if I start growing on my own soon?

Mom: It's a gamble to wait, and I'm not gambling with your health. Period.

Big surprise—Mom overruled me.

As if on cue, she waddles back into the waiting room. Nurse Susan comes to get us a few minutes later. Mom holds out her hands and I give her a pull out of her seat.

"When are you due?" the nurse asks Mom as we walk down the hall.

"December tenth."

"How wonderful! An early Christmas present. Do you have any names picked out?"

Before Mom can give her stock answer ("We're working on it"), I jump in. "I nicknamed her Boo."

The nurse smiles. "That's an interesting choice. How'd you come up with that?"

"She was a surprise," I explain.

Mom blushes. She wasn't a fan of me calling the baby Boo at first, but then Paul liked it, and it grew on her.

The three of us stop in a tiny room where the nurse weighs and measures me. And remeasures. Then measures again. "The doctor needs an exact number so we triple check," the nurse explains. Afterward, she takes us to an exam room. Mom and I don't have to wait long for the doctor to walk in.

"Nice to see you again, Felix," Dr. Ryan says as he washes his hands. "How are you?"

"Still vertically challenged," I tell him, and we both laugh. I'm not wearing it today, but I have a T-shirt that has VERTICALLY CHALLENGED on it. Actually, I have a whole collection of funny shirts that have to do with being short that Mom and other people have given me or that I've found online. My favorite one says NO, I'M NOT AN ELF.

Dr. Ryan has me climb up on the exam table as he looks through my file. I hate the way the thin paper that's covering the table makes so much noise.

"Let's see how you're doing, shall we?" he says to me.

First, he uses a thin red tape to measure my head, arms, and legs until I feel like a prize fish. Then he does the usual doctor stuff—checking my nose and throat and listening to my heart. He has me lie down on the table and pulls down the top of my underwear and takes a peek. He peeks at my armpits, too. He's looking for hair. Even though he's a doctor, my ears and cheeks get warm.

Dr. Ryan helps me sit upright.

"Everything looks good," he tells Mom. "Felix hasn't had any height growth, but he's gained two pounds."

I don't care about the two pounds *or* the fact that I didn't grow. But Mom's shoulders sag.

"Don't worry," Dr. Ryan tells her. "He's only been on treatment for a month. We often see other signs of growth first. Like needing new shoes or an increased appetite."

He opens my file. "What was our projected height?" Dr. Ryan asks, but it's more to himself.

He looks up at Mom. "How tall are you?" She tells him.

"And Dad?"

Dr. Ryan and I both wait. The question seems to have surprised Mom. After a pause, she gives him an answer.

"Hmm. That's on the short side for an adult male," Dr. Ryan says. "Refresh my memory, any history of growth disorders on his side of the family?"

"Not that we know of," Mom says.

Mom and Dr. Ryan start talking numbers and how tall I would be predicted to be if I wasn't low in the growth hormone department. But I'm not really paying attention.

All I can think about is how I know *something* about my dad now.

He's short, too.

3

IN THE DARK

"We almost forgot," Mom says as she stands in my bedroom doorway later that night. She's waving my medicine pen.

Normally, I get my shot before I head upstairs to bed. It's easier that way since the alcohol wipes and needles are in the kitchen cabinet and the pen has to stay in the refrigerator.

Mom sits on the edge of my bed. "I think we're on the right hip," she says. We rotate my growth hormone shots in the back of my upper arms, thighs, stomach, and butt. (For the record, when Mom says "hip," she really means upper butt cheek.)

I roll over and pull my pajama bottoms down just enough. My medicine comes in a pen that looks like a marker. You put a new needle on each time and then twist the dial on the opposite end of the pen to the right dose to get ready. Mom's already done that, so she swabs me with an alcohol wipe.

"The wipes are cold," I complain.

"Sorry," Mom says. "It is what it is."

Mom used to be more apologetic when I first started getting shots. She was worried she was doing it wrong and hurting me. But now we're both used to the process. The needle is small, and, to be honest, I can hardly feel it going in.

Mom pinches my skin. "Ready? One, two, three," she says. Then she pushes the needle in and presses the button on top of the pen. She leaves the needle in, and we wait ten seconds like we're supposed to. When she's done, I roll back over.

"You were awfully quiet tonight. Everything okay?" Mom asks.

"Just thinking about stuff," I say.

I immediately realize my mistake. If you tell an adult you're thinking about stuff, they're going to ask you about it.

"Like what?" Mom wants to know.

I'm not sure what to tell her. Ever since Dr. Ryan said my dad was short for a grown man, my head has been full of questions. Like, does my dad like being short? Does he make jokes or wear funny T-shirts about being short like I do? When Dr. Ryan asked Mom if there was any family history of growth disorders, she said no. But maybe my dad had growth hormone deficiency and didn't know it. Are other people in his family short, too?

But it's more than about him being short. It's the everything-else-I-don't-know-about-him part. There's probably loads of other interesting things about him.

"Are you worried about what Dr. Ryan said?" Mom asks. "Because you shouldn't be. Like he explained, it's only been a month. It can take a bit of time to see growth."

"I don't care about that."

Mom isn't giving up. "Are your classes okay?"

"Yes," I tell her.

"Because I know starting middle school can be over-whelming..."

"It's fine. Really."

"Okay, then. That's good," she says, and stands up to go. "Remember, you can talk to me about anything."

She's at the door when I realize that I *do* want to talk. "For real?" I ask. "Anything?"

Mom leans against the doorway. "Of course, buddy. What's on your mind?"

There's no good way to do this. I might as well cannonball into the deep end and hope I don't drown.

"My dad," I say.

"Felix—" Mom starts. But I interrupt.

"You told Dr. Ryan he's short."

"Yes," she says. "I did." The fact that she hasn't turned around and left yet gives me courage.

"Why didn't you ever tell me that?" I ask. "Why haven't you told me *anything* about him?"

Mom folds her arms on top of her Boo belly. "Because there's not much to tell."

"When Dr. Ryan asked about a family history of growth disorders, you said 'Not that we know of.' How do you know?"

Mom shifts her weight. "I have your father's family's med-ical history," she finally says.

"How?"

Mom doesn't answer.

"Tell me something else," I say.

"Felix..."

"I don't care what."

"Okay. Fine." She takes a deep breath. "If it'll help satisfy your curiosity for now, the two of us met when I was a sophomore in college. In an anthropology class. He graduated a year ahead of me. He was a good guy but he wasn't ready to be a father."

"Why don't I see him?"

"Felix, I don't want to get into this right now. I'll tell you all about him someday."

"When?"

Mom frowns. "I don't know. But not now."

"Why not? Is he in the Witness Protection Program?"

Mom tilts her head and gives me an amused look. "I certainly hope not."

I give her my best *I'm waiting* expression.

She sighs. "Look, I've had a long day. I'm tired and my back is killing me. Enough with the questions. It's a school night."

With that, she flips off my light and leaves me in the dark. I lie in bed and make a mental list of everything I know about my dad.

He's short.

He took an anthropology class in college.

He's a little older than Mom.

He's a good guy. (And probably not in the Witness Protection Program.)

He wasn't ready to be a father when I was born.

This last one spins around my brain like a dust devil. That was eleven years ago. Is my dad ready to be father *now*?

Wait. Does he have other kids besides me?

Mom told me what she did because she hoped it would satisfy my curiosity. But it's like the time I begged her to let me go on the Monster, a spinning octopus-looking ride at Cedar Point. She warned me it would make me dizzy and sick to my stomach, and that I'd get squished against the seat. But I didn't care. I went with her anyway.

Up. Down. Spinning around.

I almost threw up afterward. Mom asked me if I was done for the day.

But I only wanted more.

4

GREEN

*I take a break to wipe a paint smudge off my arm.
Painting Boo's room isn't how I wanted to spend
my Saturday afternoon. (Ray and I had a whole
day of online video games planned.) But Mom
wants to paint while the weather is warm enough
to open the windows and air everything out.*

"What color is this again?" I ask Paul.

"It's called Wishful Green," Mom answers from her desig-
nated spot, a chair in the hallway. She has to supervise from
there because of the paint fumes.

"As in we *wish* the nursery was done already," Paul
stage-whispers, and gives me a wink.

"I heard that," Mom says.

I roll my eyes. I'm with Paul on this one. Boo's room is taking forever. It's Mom's fault, too. She keeps changing her mind
about the wall color. She read an article in a parenting maga-
zine about how color can affect the mood of babies. But how
many moods could Boo have? From what I've heard, all she's
going to do for the first few months is eat, sleep, cry, and poop.

A glob of paint falls off the end of Paul's paintbrush and barely lands on the tarp.

"Crap! That was close," he says.

Mom clears her throat. She doesn't like the word *crap*. She thinks it's not much better than...well, another word Paul used to say. He stopped saying that word when he started hanging around me.

When Mom's not looking, Paul gives me his *Uh-oh. I'm in trouble* look. And I point at him to let him know *Better you than me.*

"Maybe I should suggest interior painter for my next Try Guy segment," Paul says. Try Guy is his shorthand for the feature he does on TV. Mom and Paul met when Paul filled in for the mascot at a Columbus Clippers baseball game three summers ago. Mom stopped a foul ball from hitting my head and afterward Paul (dressed up as Lou Seal) brought her a glove and me a batting helmet. They showed everything on the video scoreboard and it went viral for a few weeks.

Paul holds out his paint cup from the ladder. "Can you pour me more paint, please? I don't feel like climbing down again."

I'm glad to take a break. I've been sitting on the floor doing the lower parts, and my legs need a stretch.

The nursery furniture is crammed in the middle of the room so it doesn't get messed up. This used to be the room where I kept my video game console and beanbag.

"Where am I supposed to put my stuff?" I asked Mom when she told me they were kicking me out.

"Put it in your room," Mom said. "It'll fit."

"No, it won't."

"Yes, it will," Mom said. "Try."

"What if it doesn't?" I asked her. But what I really wanted to ask her was *Where am I going to fit?* And I didn't only mean in my room.

I edge my way around Boo's things.

"Be careful," Mom warns as I make my way past Furniture Island again. "That lamp used to belong to you."

She nods at a short lamp on the dresser. The base has a smiling rabbit carved out of wood. "It was the first thing I bought for you," Mom tells me. "I used it to feed and change you and rock you in the middle of the night. It wasn't too bright and it wasn't too dim. It was just right."

"Maybe we should call it the Goldilocks lamp," Paul says, and then laughs at his own joke.

"I thought it was packed away in my baby box," I say to Mom.

"It was, but it doesn't seem right to have a nursery without it."

"It doesn't seem right to take something without asking, either," I say before I can stop my mouth.

Mom frowns. "I didn't think you'd mind. I'm sorry."

I feel ashamed. What kind of big brother am I going to be if I'm not even willing to share a stupid rabbit lamp?

After I refill Paul's container, I go back to painting along the floorboards. A few minutes later, Mom announces, "Hey. I've got another name we can add to the list."

Oh, no. Not the list.

Besides not being able to pick a nursery color, Mom and Paul can't decide on a baby name.

"What about Grace?" Mom says.

"Hmmm. Maybe," Paul says.

In the two years he and Mom have been married, I've learned that whenever Paul says "Hmmm, maybe," it means he doesn't like it and is being nice.

"What about Rose?" Paul suggests.

"Nope," Mom says. "I knew a Rose in high school. She was mean."

"What about Claudia?" I suggest. "Like from that book where the kids live in the museum." (Which, for the record, could never happen nowadays.)

No response.

After a few moments, Mom says, "My favorite is still Hunter."

Hunter is a variation of Huntington. As in Huntington Park, the ballfield where Mom and Paul met and where Paul proposed.

"What do you think, Felix?" Mom asks.

"Hunter is good," I say.

"Just good?" Mom says playfully. "This is going to be your sister's name forever. It's got to be great."

I don't know what Mom wants me to say. They didn't like my suggestion. Besides, picking a baby name doesn't seem like a sibling thing. It's a mom and dad thing. I wonder if my dad helped choose my name.

I've been thinking about him ever since the appointment and my conversation with Mom that night. It seems strange that I don't have a photograph. I don't even know his name or where he lives or what kinds of things he likes to do. I wonder if he ever thinks about me.

Paul throws out another idea.

"I knew a girl named Holly when I was a kid," he says.

"Ha. Ha. Very funny. I'm not naming our daughter Holly Woods," Mom tells him.

Woods is Paul's last name. Mom kept our last name when they got married. That way, she and I would still have the same last name. But Boo will have Paul's last name.

"Ooo. I've got one." Paul sounds excited. "How about Elizabeth?"

"I'll add it to the list," Mom says. "We could call her Lizzy."

"Yeah, but I knew a girl in fourth grade who got called Frizzy Lizzy," says Paul. "So that won't work if she inherits my curls."

"Or my red hair," Mom says.

"Oh, man. Can you imagine if the poor thing gets both?" Paul replies. "She'll look like Little Orphan Annie."

I try to picture what a baby with curly red hair would look like.

My hair is straight. And dark brown. Last year in fifth grade, we learned about genes and why we look the way we do. Having red hair is a recessive, or nondominant, gene. This means I probably got my dark hair from my dad.

I wonder what else I inherited from my dad. Boo won't have to guess about stuff like that. She'll know what both of her biological parents look like. (Considering I don't look like either of them, she probably won't look related to me at all.)

Is it possible to be jealous of a baby?

5

WELCOME TO ALBUQUERQUE

It feels strange to be going to school on a Sunday afternoon. But today is the Club and Sports Fair.

"Have fun," Paul says as I climb out of the car. Mom tells me they'll be back to pick me up after they run some errands. I'm glad they're not coming in with me. There are a few parents and kids with their younger brothers and sisters in tow, but mostly it's students.

Ray is already here, waiting for me by the front door.

The hallway isn't as crowded as it is during breaks between periods, but it's busy. Ray and I almost get trampled by a pack of eighth graders who don't seem to care that they're hogging the hall. We press ourselves against the wall to let them pass and I notice that we're directly across from the teachers' lounge. The door window is covered with Christmas wrapping paper so you can't see in.

"That's weird," I say, pointing.

"Maybe that's the only wrapping paper they could find," Ray says.

22

When we get to the gym, there's a sign taped to the door: WELCOME TO ALBUQUERQUE.

I'm about to ask Ray what he thinks it means, but he's already inside.

The gym has rows of tables with signs for various clubs and sports you can sign up for. Ray and I start at the table to the left and make our way around. We stop and check out a few tables and listen to the student representatives and faculty advisors talk about their groups.

"I like your shirt," the teacher at the Cooking Club table says when we walk by.

I'm wearing my YOU GOTTA HAND IT TO SHORT PEOPLE (BECAUSE THEY USUALLY CAN'T REACH ANYWAY) one today. "Thanks," I say.

"Do you like cooking?" the teacher asks.

"Nope," Ray says. "But I like eating."

The teacher smiles. "What about you?" she asks me.

I tell her I do. Mom and I used to experiment in the kitchen on the weekends sometimes. We'd open a cookbook to a page and make whatever recipe was there. We called them Random Recipe Days.

"Well, you should think about joining, then," the teacher says. I do, but only for half a second. The Cooking Club probably uses the home ec room. What if I needed a step stool to reach the counters and cabinets? It would be a real-life version of my shirt every day.

"Hmm. Maybe," I say, borrowing Paul's go-to response when he wants to get out of something.

We move on to the History Club table. Since the person there is busy talking to other students, we check out the Civil War display. Someone's snuck a Lego Darth Vader in with the soldier figurines, which is funny. I'll have to remember to tell Paul about it.

"Hey," Ray says, pulling on my elbow. "Look."

A few tables down there's a kid throwing a yo-yo. We walk over and watch.

"I didn't know there was a Yo-Yo Club," I say.

"Me neither," Ray says.

The kid grabs two yo-yos off the table and hands them to me and Ray. "Here," he says. "Let me show you how to do a trick called Walk the Dog."

We watch what the boy is doing and give it a couple of tries. Ray gets it, but I can't.

"Don't worry," the kid says. "Keep practicing and by the time you get to middle school, you'll be able to do it."

"I *am* in middle school," I tell him. "Sixth grade."

"Really? Uh, sorry," he says. "I thought you were his little brother."

I shrug. "I skipped two grades." I manage to keep a straight face, but Ray cracks up.

"For real?" the yo-yo kid asks.

"Nah," I admit. "It's just fun to say."

The kid holds his hand out for a fist bump and says, "Good one. You got me."

Ray and I decide to split up, since he wants to find some kind of art-related club to join and I want to see what else there is.

Robotics League. Cross-country. Theater. Math Club. (I wonder if Ray even bothered to check it out. I'm guessing he did so he could at least tell his dad he considered it.) Nothing is really grabbing my attention. After a while, I decide to go find Ray, stopping for a drink from the water fountain in the hall first.

On the way, I'm distracted by a table that has poster board

with a giant question mark on it. The teacher sitting there waves me over.

"Hi. I'm Mr. Stockfish," he says, and extends his hand for me to shake. "Are you up for a quick quiz?"

"You mean like a survey or something?" I ask.

He smiles. "Not exactly. More of a 'How good a witness are you?' kind of thing."

Ray slides up to the table next to me. "Here you are," he says to me. "What's this club?" he asks.

Mr. Stockfish goes through his spiel again, and Ray and I tell him we're game.

The first question on the quiz is:

There was a sign on the gym door. It said "Welcome to _____."

That one's easy.

We keep going. There are twelve questions in all. About the wrapping paper on the teachers' lounge door. About the song that was played over the loudspeaker ("Take Me Out to the Ball Game"—I remember because it made me think of Paul dressing up as the mascot), and what kind of animal pin Principal Good was wearing on her sweater (a peacock—it had really long feathers).

I got ten out of the twelve questions right. Ray got ten, too, but he missed different questions than I did.

"Nicely done," Mr. Stockfish tells us.

"Do we win a prize or something?" I ask.

He laughs. "No. But I *will* tell you about the Forensic Science Club. It's a group of kids who get together and work in teams to solve staged crimes using forensic science techniques."

"Like the *CSI* shows on TV? Fingerprints and blood spatters, stuff like that?" Ray asks.

"Well, there's more to solving crimes than those things, but yes, like the *CSI* shows. Here. Check this out," Mr. Stockfish says, pulling a diorama out from under the table.

It's a model of the upstairs hallway with miniature lockers and dolls for people. (I know it's the upstairs hallway because I recognize the foreign languages posters.) It's super detailed. And even the tiny lights on the ceiling work.

"Did you make this?" Ray asks.

Mr. Stockfish beams. "I did! I was inspired by the god-mother of forensic science, Frances Glessner Lee. She created detailed crime scene dioramas in the 1940s. They were called the Nutshell Studies of Unexplained Death and they're still used to train people to study crime scenes."

"Would we get to make our own if we join the club?" Ray asks.

"That's a great idea," Mr. Stockfish tells him. "I'll definitely have to see if we can work that out."

Ray is hooked. He likes drawing best, but he's up for any kind of art. Last year, when we had to make clay Dr. Seuss houses in art, he spent two extra weeks perfecting his before he let the teacher fire it in the kiln.

"Study the scene," Mr. Stockfish tells us, nodding toward the box. "I call this the Case of the Unclaimed Backpack. Can you figure out who the backpack belongs to?"

Ray and I lean in closer and study the scene. There's a backpack on the floor, in the middle of the hall. It's partly open and a moldy sandwich is sticking out. The teacher doll has her hands up in the air as if she's asking, *Whose smelly backpack is this?*

There's a taller boy and a shorter boy. Each one is pointing to the other person.

Hmm. The open lockers don't seem to give anything away. . . . Oh! I smile and straighten up.

"Got it?" Mr. Stockfish asks.

"Already?" Ray says.

"The backpack belongs to that guy," I say, pointing at the taller kid.

"How do you know?"

"Because of the straps on the backpack. They're pulled all the way out. If the short kid wore that bag, it would practically bang the back of his knees."

Mr. Stockfish gives me a thumbs-up. "You're right. Good catch. Having an eye for details is important in solving crimes. You might enjoy the club. It's brand-new this year, and we're going to investigate the mysteries of the world." He says this last part dramatically. Then he switches back to a normal voice. "Or at least some fake crime scenes at Orange Middle School."

"We should sign up," Ray says to me. "Come on. *CSI*, investigating, looking for evidence, solving mysteries and all that."

I've already got a mystery in my life: my dad.

It's clear that Mom isn't going to tell me anything anytime soon. But I want to know more. Even just his name. It isn't fair Boo will know both of her parents.

Maybe the Forensic Science Club is exactly what I need to help me find him.

"We start this Wednesday," Mr. Stockfish says. "Then beginning next week, meetings will be on Mondays and Wednesdays. Three-thirty to five."

I grab the pencil Mr. Stockfish is holding out and write my name on the sign-up sheet.

6

GUINEA PIGS

*Forensic Science Club meets in Mr. Stockfish's biology
room in the eighth-grade hall. I readjust my backpack
on my shoulder as I take the stairs and wish I'd saved
the apple from my lunch. Dr. Ryan was right about
me being hungrier than I used to be before the shots.*

Instead of desks, the classroom has tall tables with stools
around each of them.

"Hey," Ray calls from the other side of the room. He's
wearing a shirt from the summer art camp he begged to go to
last year. I make my way over and climb onto a stool.

"What did your dad say when you told him you joined this
instead of Math Club?" I ask. (I've forgotten to ask this on the
bus the last few days.)

"He wasn't happy. But I told him he'd have to deal."

Ray laughs at my expression. "I'm kidding. I didn't really
say that. But I told him Math Club met on Fridays and I have
clarinet lessons on Fridays."

"You lied?"

Ray shrugs.

"What if he finds out?"

"He won't. He can't even list the classes I'm taking. I doubt he'll bother to find out which club meets on which days."

Paul is the kind of parent that knows *everything*. Even the names of my doctors and stupid stuff like what I was for my first Halloween. (A dinosaur.) He even came to my training appointment and learned how to give me my growth hormone shot in case Mom couldn't.

I wonder if I could ever get away with lying to Paul about something big.

Ray and I check out the rest of the group. There are around a dozen kids, but school only got out ten minutes ago and people are straggling in. Seems like an equal mix of sixth, seventh, and eighth graders. One of the other sixth graders here is Casey, the girl who sits in front of me and Ray on the bus. She sees us and gives us a peace sign.

"All right," Mr. Stockfish says a few minutes later. "It appears most of the Testudines have arrived."

The room is like, *Um, what?*

"Sorry," he goes on. "Just a little biology teacher humor. If you don't know what I'm talking about, wonderful! You'll have a chance to look it up later and learn something."

Mr. Stockfish welcomes us to the first-ever official meeting of the school's Forensic Science Club and thanks us for signing up to be guinea pigs. (This gets snickers.) Next, he passes out name tags and markers so we can write the name we prefer to go by. He tells us he prefers the Great and Powerful Mr. Stockfish.

"More teacher humor," he says. "Mr. S is fine."

He goes over what we can expect for the next few months. Along with hearing about what different types of forensic scientists do, we'll be learning how to secure and photograph a crime scene and collect and analyze evidence like fingerprints, hair, and footprints. There might be a couple of guest speakers, too.

"And what's the use of learning something if you can't apply it?" Mr. S says. "We'll be visiting mock crime scenes, where you'll have the chance to use what we're learning to investigate and solve a crime."

This gets the room buzzing.

Mr. S holds up his hand. "I knew that would get everyone's attention," he says. "But there's more! At the end of the semester, all four middle schools in our district are having an interschool tournament. One team from each will be chosen to represent their school, and there will be prizes. Okay. Not prizes. But there will be trophies! Lemme hear you ooh and aah."

Everyone laughs but also oohs and aahs like we were told. (Note to self: Sign up for Mr. Stockfish's biology class when I'm in eighth grade.)

Mr. S claps his hands and rubs them together. "So. Next order of business—our club motto."

He flips on the SMART Board behind him and reads aloud.

To a great mind, nothing is little. —Sherlock Holmes

"What does that mean?" he asks us. "Anyone want to hazard a guess?"

No hands go up.

"Hold up. Before we go any further," Mr. S says, "everyone's on the same page that Sherlock Holmes is a fictional character, correct? If you don't know who created him, there's another thing to look up and learn. All right then. Our motto. Any guesses?"

A girl near the front raises her hand. "It means everything is important?"

Mr. S smiles and throws his hands up like he's celebrating. "Close enough!"

The girl exhales.

"The quote means that if you're wise, you understand that paying attention to details is important. This is especially true when you're solving crimes.

"And to make sure you remember this," Mr. S tells us, "we're going to have some fun."

He explains that he's going to put us into four teams of four using a specific detail.

"For example, maybe you all have alien tattoos," Mr. S says. "Only it won't be that since none of you are, in fact, sporting a tattoo of an alien"—he pauses to look around slowly—"that I'm *aware* of."

This gets a laugh from everybody.

Mr. S. continues. "Your first task as a team will be to figure out why you were grouped together. Now, everyone up."

7

SHORTLOCK HOLMES

We get up and stand to one side of the room.
Mr. S moves around, sorting students into groups.

When he's done, I'm on a team with Ray, Casey, and Priya, the girl who raised her hand when Mr. S asked about the club motto.

Priya immediately takes charge. "First, we should introduce ourselves and say what grade we're in."

It turns out Priya is in sixth grade like the rest of us. But we don't think it's that simple, since Mr. S said it would be something that wasn't obvious.

"We need to take notes," Priya says. "Anyone got paper and a pencil?"

Ray grabs the small sketchbook and pencil he carries in his backpack.

Priya nods in approval. "Okay," she says. "The first rule of science: Assess, then progress."

The three of us look at her. "Well, it's *my* first rule anyway. It means, let's look at what we already know, and then go from there. I'm going to be a medical examiner and they do things in order."

"You want to be a medical examiner?" Casey asks. "Like a doctor who investigates dead bodies?"

Priya looks like she's ready for a fight. "Yes," she says. "What's wrong with that?"

"Nothing," Casey says. "It's brilliant!" I'm not sure Ray and I would use that particular adjective (*brilliant* is one of Casey's favorite words), but we nod vigorously in agreement. Priya's face and shoulders relax.

Ray finds a clean sheet of paper and writes: *Why did Mr. S put us together?* at the top. Then he adds a *POSSIBILITIES* and a *NO* column.

We begin looking for connections. Two of us are wearing jeans (me and Ray). Casey and Priya are in shorts. And three of us are wearing long-sleeved T-shirts. (Mine is a short-sleeved one that says TRAVEL SIZE.) There doesn't seem to be anything special about our clothes. They don't have matching colors or patterns.

Under the *NO* column on his data sheet, Ray writes: *clothes*. Under the *POSSIBILITIES* column, he writes: *We're all in 6th grade.*

Casey studies everyone's head. "Well, it's not hair color since you guys have dark hair and mine is lighter."

"Hair length?" Ray suggests. But that doesn't seem right, either, since our hair is different lengths. He adds it to our *NO* list.

"We need to brainstorm. Nothing is off-limits," Priya says.

The four of us sit down at a table to think. Ray keeps track of our ideas.

Number of pockets.
Type of shoe.
None of us are wearing braces.
Height. (That one clearly isn't it since everyone else is a foot taller than I am.)
Number of syllables in our names.

But after a while, the ideas get more far-fetched. Ray writes them down, too.

None of us got here late.
We all hate mint ice cream. (This last one came up because Priya is wearing a shirt with a local ice cream shop's logo.)

"Come on," Priya says after I say the ice cream one. "How would Mr. S know that? It has to be something *observable*."

Two of the other teams have figured out why they were put together. That leaves two teams, including us, and there's only twenty minutes left.

Ray taps his pencil. I wiggle my foot. Priya gets up from the table and starts pacing. Casey chews on her thumbnail.

The clock is ticking and we have nothing.

Since my feet don't reach the footrest bar, my legs are starting to feel weird from dangling off the stool. I climb down and sit against a wall on the floor to give them a break.

"You okay?" Casey asks from her stool.

"Yeah." My stomach growls. *Man, I'm hungry.*

Casey's backpack is on the floor next to the table. Maybe I could ask if she has a bag of pretzels or a pack of cookies or something. She'd probably share if I asked. She's nice like that. Her socks even have smiley faces on them and say HAVE A NICE DAY.

Hold up. I've got it!

I'm on my feet in a flash.

"Our clothes," I tell the group.

"That's already under *NO*," Ray says.

"No. Not the color or pattern," I tell everyone. "Look. We each have some kind of writing on our clothes."

Everyone looks. First at their own clothes and then at each other's clothes. Ray is wearing his art camp shirt. Priya's in her ice cream shop shirt. Me in my TRAVEL SIZE T-shirt.

When Casey frowns, I point at her socks.

The four of us walk-run up to Mr. S's desk and give him our guess. "Nicely done, team," he says.

Casey, Ray, Priya, and I high-five each other on the way back to our table.

"We rock," Ray says. Then he turns to me and says, "I'm proud of you." The two of us crack up while the girls try to figure out what's so funny.

"Yeah, Felix." Casey smiles. "You're a regular Shortlock Holmes."

I like that. Shortlock Holmes sounds like someone who always gets his guy.

Or probably does.

8

TURTLE

It's Friday night and Mom tricked me. She said we were going out to eat, but then Paul pulled the car into the parking lot of a store called Oh Baby!

"We're going to make a quick stop," Mom says. "It'll be fast. I promise."

Mom is anything but fast these days, but I don't say a word.

"We're on a mission for a crib," Paul says. "And that's it. It's the only piece of furniture we don't have."

But the second we walk through the doors, Paul gets distracted. He moves from thing to thing, like a kid in a toy store. "I'm not exactly sure what this is," he says, holding up a box that says DIAPER GENIE. "And yet we definitely need it."

Mom laughs and reminds him that there'll be a baby shower.

I wonder if my dad was this goofy when Mom was pregnant with me. But then I think about what Mom said about him not being ready to be a father. Was he at least the tiniest bit excited when he found out?

I remember when Mom and Paul told me they were having a baby. Actually, Mom said "we're" having a baby. As in the three of us. Like it was some kind of family decision.

We'd gone out for brunch because it was Mother's Day. Mom and Paul were acting weird. All giggly and smiley. After Mom opened the gift I gave her (a vase that Paul helped pick out), she pulled a wrapped package out of her bag.

"I know it's Mother's Day," she said, "but what I want most is for you to have this."

It was a shirt. It said: OLDEST.

"Do you know what it means?" Paul asked when I didn't say anything right away.

I looked at Mom. "You're having a baby."

"No," she said, "*we're* having a baby."

"On purpose?" I asked.

Mom's smile drooped. Paul jumped in. "It was a happy surprise. Kind of neat, huh?"

"Are you excited?" Mom asked.

I wasn't sure what I was. I wasn't *not* excited. But I was used to being an only child.

Mom was looking at me expectantly. Plus, it was Mother's Day. So I said, "That's awesome. I can't wait."

That must have been the right answer, or close enough, because Mom beamed. Then she and Paul started talking about how happy they were that I finally knew the secret. (It wasn't a secret for that much longer; four days later they put an official *Surprise—we're expecting!* announcement online.)

At least they skipped doing a big gender reveal thing. Paul wanted to wait to find out, but Mom said it was more practical to know because then you can buy clothes.

And buying clothes is exactly what Mom did. It got to the

point where we couldn't go into a store without checking out the baby department.

Oh Baby! is like a whole warehouse of baby departments.

Mom and Paul ask me which crib I like, but I don't have an opinion. I'm pretty sure Boo won't have an opinion, either, though I don't say this out loud. I don't get why Mom and Paul are worried about this kind of stuff. Or how they can fuss over Boo so much before she's even born. She's not a person yet. She's not even a baby. She's a bump.

I think Mom can tell I'm not interested in the crib mission because she says, "Felix, can you do me a favor?"

"Sure."

"Boo will need a blanket to come home with. Will you go pick one out?"

I don't know how picking out a blanket is any more fun than picking out a crib, but I walk over to the blankets like Mom asked.

Holy Toledo. There's a whole aisle of just blankets.

White ones. Yellow ones. Green ones. Blue and pink ones. Big ones, small ones. Blankets that are fuzzy. Blankets with things like ducks, trucks, or bunnies on them.

My head is about to explode.

I check out a few of the blankets up close. They're super soft, but the flannel ones feel best. They're the type of blanket I'd like, so I look for one of those.

I've got a yellow one with birds on it in my hand and I'm on my way back to the crib aisle when another blanket catches my eye.

It's extra soft. The background is white. And it has baby turtles with different shades of green shells. Testudines.

That's the scientific name for turtles, and what Mr. S called the latecomers. I looked it up after I got home from the Forensic Science Club meeting. It's perfect.

Mom loves the blanket, even though it's not pink or super girly. "I love it," she says when I show her. "Turtles! It's like you're saying it feels like she's taking forever to arrive."

Mom tears up and Paul hands her a tissue.

For the record, Mom's wrong. The reason I picked the blanket was because I want Boo to slow down and take her time in getting here.

9

THE SCENE OF THE CRIME

*On Monday, Mr. S introduces a few new people
who've joined Forensic Science Club. Even though
there's only three of them, Mr. S makes them
their own team.*

"No worries, Mr. S," a kid named Tomás says. "We won't even
need a fourth person."

It seems like an overly confident thing to say. But I know
Tomás from my neighborhood. He's an eighth grader and he
acts like someone who's used to winning stuff.

This new group makes five teams. It's more competition
to represent the school at the tournament, but I think Ray,
Casey, Priya, and I are in good shape. Especially after how well
we worked together at the first meeting.

"Today we're discussing the first step in crime scene investigation," Mr. S begins. "Which, not surprisingly, is determin-
ing what exactly *is* the crime scene."

This makes me think of Priya's first rule. Assess, then
progress.

Mr. S sketches the layout of a house on the board and labels the rooms. Out of the corner of my eye, I can see the fingers on Ray's right hand twitch. I bet he's dying to get out his sketchbook. "My dad sees numbers in his head," Ray once told me. "I see shapes."

Mr. S finishes up his house on the board and goes on with the introduction. "Let's say, for example, there's been a robbery. Someone broke into a victim's house and then broke into the safe in their office. The primary crime scene is the office. But what other areas might be considered part of the crime scene? Where else could we look for evidence?"

Everyone brainstorms: the hallway leading to the office, the rooms next to the office, the whole house, the front porch, the yard, the street.

"Identifying where to look helps the police and the forensic team secure the area and keep evidence protected from being lost or contaminated," Mr. S says. "After we've established where to search, the next step is to locate and identify the evidence."

Mr. S goes over the process, step by step. At the end, he announces that we're taking a field trip.

"Slow your roll," he tells us when we react. "It's a walking field trip. To the cafeteria." Mr. S passes out worksheets, note cards, and plastic baggies, and tells us to grab a clipboard from the bin by the door. (Ray gets his sketchbook out of his backpack.)

"No simian behavior in the halls," he warns us as we file out of the biology room.

I'm fairly sure he means "No monkey business."

There's yellow CAUTION tape and a sign that says CLOSED:

41

INVESTIGATION IN PROGRESS outside the cafeteria door. It's a nice touch.

The cafeteria is where the school has plays and band concerts, so there's a raised stage off to one side. Including the stage, the area is divided into five sections by masking tape on the floor. Mr. S assigns each team to a section to find and properly collect evidence that he's planted.

Our team gets the stage.

Casey, Priya, and Ray place their hands on the apron of the stage and push themselves up onto it.

"Need a hand?" Casey asks when she notices I haven't budged.

"No," I tell her, and raise my hand twelve inches over my head. "I need a foot."

Casey and Priya laugh. "Ha! I get it," Casey says. Ray's heard that joke a bunch of times already.

I use the stairs and join my team.

"You guys check that side for evidence," Priya tells me and Casey. "We'll take the other side."

Casey and I find our first piece of evidence, a shoe, and write down its description like we're supposed to: black tennis shoe, men's size nine. (Mom took me to get bigger shoes the other night. But I have a long way to go before I wear that size.)

"What letter are we on?" Casey asks Priya, who's keeping track of the evidence labels.

"E," Priya calls from the other side of the stage.

Casey folds a note card in half and writes E on it and puts it down to mark the spot next to the shoe, and we use our cell phones to take a picture.

"Why are you so short, anyway?" Casey says. "Is there something wrong with you?"

The question throws me off. I've been asked this, or something like it, lots of times before. But I haven't told anyone about being diagnosed with growth hormone deficiency. Not even Ray. For the most part, he and everyone else think it's cool that I'm short. It makes me interesting. If people knew I had a disorder, I'm afraid they might think it was weird and say things like "Aww, that's too bad." Or "Leave him alone; he's sick," when I got teased. One: I'm not sick. And two: I can handle things myself.

I give Casey my go-to answer for when people ask me why I'm short. "I'm space-efficient, I guess."

"Does it bother you?" Casey asks while we work. "Being short, I mean."

This question throws me off, too. But in a good way. Nobody has ever asked me that. They just assume it does.

"No," I tell Casey. "I like it."

We go back to searching for our next bit of evidence.

"Except," I add after some thought, "when it comes to roller coasters. It would be nice to have more options."

Casey nods. "I get that. My dads make me take my little brother on the kiddie rides when we go to Cedar Point. Like, seriously? How many times can going around and around in a circle be fun?"

We find a pen with the name of a local bank on it. Somebody might have dropped it, but for all we know, it could be evidence. So we process it.

"Do you have any brothers or sisters?" Casey asks as the two of us bag the pen into evidence.

"My mom's pregnant. I'm getting a sister in a couple of months," I tell her.

"Really? That's brilliant. My brother was supposed to be a

sister. Oh, well." Casey laughs. "Marc's cool. And man, does he love those stupid rides."

I nod like I totally relate, but I don't. I can't even wrap my brain around what Boo will be like as a baby, let alone as a kid who can talk and has opinions about things like amusement park rides.

Casey keeps talking. "I've got an older sister, though. She and I have the same bio-mom."

"Bio-mom?" I ask.

"Yeah. My two dads used a surrogate. It's a friend of theirs, so Katie—that's my sister—and I know her. Marc was adopted from another woman."

I've never met someone with a half sibling before. But she didn't call Marc her half brother. Just her brother. Will it feel weird that Boo and I have different dads? I guess it might since she'll call Paul Dad and I don't.

"Hey. Sorry if this is rude, but how does that surrogate thing work?" I ask Casey. "Is it like having three parents?"

"Nope. My bio-mom signed a form that said she gave up her parental rights, so she doesn't have a legal say in our lives. But she comes over for birthdays and at Thanksgiving and Christmas, and helps out in a pinch sometimes."

What would it be like if I invited my dad over for Thanksgiving dinner? Where would he sit at the table? Every year, Mom makes us go around the table and say what we're thankful for. (It went quickly when it was only the two of us.) Would my dad say something mushy like Paul did the first year he and Mom were married? *"I'm grateful for my beautiful wife and her awesome son for allowing me to be a part of their lives."*

It's strange thinking about my dad being in my life and

sitting at that table. I haven't decided what I'll do if I actually find him, but Casey's got me thinking about it.

I'll have to find a way to convince Mom to let me go visit my dad. Or to let him visit us.

I wonder if he would come to holidays and birthdays, if I asked.

Hopefully, after a few more Forensic Science Club meetings and some investigation skills under my belt, I'll get the chance.

10

A SMALL, LITTLE PUNCTUATION MARK

I know something is up on Tuesday when Mom tells me to put on a clean shirt. We rarely go out to eat during the week.

Mom and Paul are all smiles in the car, but neither of them will give me a clue what's going on. Not even when we pull into a fancy-ish sit-down restaurant.

"It's our way of celebrating getting the nursery done. And to thank you for helping," Paul finally says. I don't buy it.

The hostess shows us to a booth. A few minutes later, our server arrives and sets down a connect-the-dots puzzle and a box of crayons in front of me. I don't mind. One time at another restaurant, a server thought I was "adorable and such a talented artist" that she brought me a free sundae. Now, whenever I get a chance, I try to score another free dessert. I turn the puzzle over and to get work drawing a super-detailed cartoon robot, like Ray showed me.

"Felix," Mom warns. But I can tell she's not that serious.

The three of us split an appetizer and chat about random

stuff. Halfway through the entrees, Mom and Paul share a look.

"So, look, buddy," Mom starts. "Paul and I would like to discuss something important with you."

Called it.

"Your sister is going to be here soon," Mom says. "And Paul and I have been talking."

When I don't say anything, she goes on. "Paul and I would like for Boo to have the same last name as Paul. If you think about it, it makes a lot of sense."

"I thought that was already decided," I say. "About her having Paul's last name, I mean."

"Yes. But then you and I would have different last names than Paul and your sister," Mom says.

She pauses.

"And that could cause confusion," Mom continues. "Therefore, I've decided—well, Paul and I have decided—that we're going to combine our last names. Boo's last name will be Fine-Woods."

Then Mom drops the bomb. "Paul and I are changing our last name to Fine-Woods, too."

It feels like I've been sucker-punched in the gut. "But then I'll be the only one in the family with a different last name," I say.

Mom clears her throat. "There's a solution to that," she says gently.

"Yeah," I say. "The solution is for you to keep our last name."

She frowns and looks to Paul for help.

"You know I love you and your mom and Boo more than anything, right?" he says. "We're a family. Look. I understand how you must feel about your mom changing her last name."

"No, you don't."

We're both startled. I've never talked back to Paul like that before.

I almost feel bad about it, but Paul swallows and continues. "That's fair. I've never been in your position, and I *don't* know how you feel. Can I tell you how I feel, though?

"I'll take your silence as an okay," he says. "I'm excited. Your mom and I have been discussing this for a while. Blending our names is a public way of acknowledging that we've blended our lives. We've—you, your mom, me, and now Boo—we've created something new. A new last name feels right."

"Not to me," I say.

Mom and Paul stare at me. I stare right back. I don't know if they're waiting for me to say something else. I do anyway. "I like my last name. It goes with my first name, and I've had it for eleven years."

"And it'll still be your last name," Mom says. "Only a bit longer. And have a small, little punctuation mark. What do you think?"

What do I think? It doesn't feel *like a small thing.*

"Fine-Woods is a stupid name. It sounds like the name of a spa."

Mom's eyes grow shiny.

Paul steps in. "We were hoping to have it taken care of before Boo came. But it doesn't look like we can. Our court date isn't until the middle of January. You have some time."

Mom covers my hand with hers. "It's your decision. We're only asking that you think about it. In the end, it's up to you."

How can they expect me to make a decision? Mom called the hyphen a small, little punctuation mark. To me, it would be way more than that.

I don't want to do it. But if I don't, I'll be the odd one out. Boo, Mom, Paul—they'll be part of a family.

And I'll be apart.

✳

Mom and Paul ordered dessert at the restaurant, but I skipped it. As soon as we got home, I went to my bedroom. I guess Mom and Paul are giving me space. It's past the time I normally get my shot and Mom hasn't even knocked on my door.

I can't believe they're hyphenating their names like it's no big deal. Did they even stop to think about how this could affect me? I like my last name. It's a part of me, just like being short. But that's not the only thing that's bothering me.

What if my dad decides to look for me someday? He might not know my first name. But he knows Mom's full name. He could look her up online.

When Mom and Paul got married, his station did a story on the wedding because they met while he was doing his Give It a Try Guy thing. That video isn't up anymore. If you do some digging, though, you can find a newspaper article about the viral video from the ballpark. And another short one about the wedding. There's also a story about the company where Mom works where she's quoted. That comes up, too, when you search her name.

Mom's not a big fan of social media. But if you tried hard enough, it wouldn't be impossible to track her down. *If* she doesn't go changing her last name to something else.

I have to do something.

Okay. January is four months away.

If my dad won't be able to find me after that, I'll just have to find him now.

11

FINGERPRINTS EVERYWHERE

Dactyloscopy.

This is what we find written on the board when we walk into Forensic Science Club the next day. Mr. S seems excited that none of us know what it means.

"Yay! Another chance to learn something new," he says. "Only this time, I won't make you look it up."

"But I just did," Tomás says, waving his cell phone.

Mr. S grins. "Well, don't keep everyone in suspense. Knowledge is power, my good man."

"It's the study of fingerprint identification," Tomás announces.

With that, Mr. S launches into his lesson.

"Fingerprints are made up of ridges and grooves that form a pattern. They're unique," he tells us. "No one in the entire world has the same fingerprints. Not even identical twins. And your fingerprints will remain the same your entire life.

Even if you get a cut or a burn, the effects on your prints are usually temporary. Your fingerprints will grow back on the healed skin."

Mr. S explains the different types of patterns and puts examples up on the SMART Board. The whorl patterns, especially the accidental whorl, remind me of those swirling pictures of outer space. Casey agrees with me. But Ray and Priya think they look like Vincent van Gogh's *The Starry Night.* "I should know," Ray insists. "I researched van Gogh for the Wax Museum thing we did last year."

Either way, it's kind of cool we can have galaxies, or starry nights, at the tips of our fingers.

Someone asks if people in the same families can have similar fingerprint patterns.

"Well, again," Mr. S says, "no one has identical fingerprints. But yes, family members can have similar patterns."

Maybe Boo and I will have fingerprints that look alike. That would be *something,* even if I'm the only one with a different last name.

"Felix," Ray whispers. "You good?"

I don't know how to explain what's going on to Ray. He complains about his dad and thinks I'm lucky to have Paul. He'd wonder why I was bothering to look for my dad in the first place. Or why I cared if my dad wanted to find me. It's probably easier not to tell him anything.

"Yeah," I tell Ray, and refocus on what we're doing. I need all the investigation skills I can get.

Mr. S passes out balloons and gives each table an ink pad to share. Everyone is supposed to blow up a balloon ("About the size of your fist," Mr. S says) but not tie it. We're supposed to have someone hold it while we press our thumbs onto the ink pad and then the balloon.

"What's the next step in the procedure?" Ray asks after he's made his print.

Priya consults her notes. "Give the balloon a few more breaths and tie it off."

The four of us take turns helping each other with the balloons and ink. When you blow the balloon up, you can see your fingerprint in detail. We compare our prints to the examples to see which pattern we have.

"Anyone have a tented arch?" Mr. S asks.

I raise my hand.

"Awesome! That's the rarest pattern. Only five to ten percent of the population has that."

"Cool. I'm rare," I say.

"Cool. I'm proud," Ray answers. And the two of us grin at our inside joke.

Mr. S explains that there are different kinds of fingerprints. Patent prints are obvious. They're made when we touch something like blood or dirt and then touch something else. Impressed prints are 3-D. They're made when we touch something soft, like dust or wax.

"And then there are latent prints," Mr. S says. "These prints are made when oil or sweat on your hands leaves a print behind. And the ones most commonly found at a crime scene. But you can't see them. When folks on TV shows and movies are dusting objects at a crime scene, that's what they're looking for."

I press my thumb against the table to see if it leaves a mark. How many other kids' fingerprints are there, too?

"Now I have a surprise for you," Mr. S says, interrupting my thoughts.

Mr. S has made each team their own crime scene tool kit. Our box has four small spiral notebooks, a box of vinyl gloves, two magnifying glasses, tweezers, baggies, a permanent marker, makeup brushes, a roll of packing tape, blank note cards, and a travel-size container with a dark powder inside.

"The black stuff is homemade fingerprint powder courtesy of the high school forensic science class," he tells us.

We start lifting fingerprints (Mr. S says that's the correct terminology) from surfaces around the room, using the makeup brushes to sprinkle fingerprint powder and then gently blowing the excess away to find latent prints. We carefully lay pieces of tape over prints to lift and tape them to the note cards. That makes the fingerprints easier to study and compare to the patterns on the board.

"Did you know medical examiners take fingerprints of dead people?" Priya says as we work. "It's to help identify them."

"Oh, yeah? That's interesting," Ray says. "I'm not sure I'd want to touch a dead body, though. That would be way weird."

"My friends think it's weird, too," Priya says softly.

Ray, Casey, and I exchange looks.

"Well, maybe not weird," Ray clarifies. "Just, um, different."

Priya's expression shifts, brightens. She suggests that we try using the glass beakers on the biology room shelf to make prints. The glass surface works really well. And soon everyone wants to try.

Mr. S says it's fine as long as we wipe off the prints afterward, like criminals. "Not that I'm telling you how to get away with a crime or anything," he says.

At the end of the club meeting, while the other teams finish cleaning up, Priya, Ray, Casey, and I sit at our table. Ray grabs the ink pad and presses the outside edge of his fist on it. Then he presses his hand on a note card. He puts five dots over that print with his pinky finger. "We worked with ink at camp," he explains as he works. Ray's dad let him go to art camp last summer because Ray agreed to go to math camp, too.

"Look," Ray says when he's done, and holds up the card. "It's a baby's foot."

"Hey, neat," Priya says. "It looks like the footprints they make in the hospital when babies are born."

"Lemme try," Casey says. I grab the ink pad after her and make my own baby's foot.

I'm admiring my work when the idea hits me.

12

HOPE

"Mom, where's my baby book?"

"I'm not sure," she says from the couch. It's Saturday and Mom's lying down, feet up, because her ankles are swollen. "Why do you need it?"

"Something for school," I lie.

Some moms ask loads of questions if you say you're working on something for school. But I learned a long time ago that my mom will let it go. She'll ask if I need help, and otherwise, she's hands off.

"I haven't seen it since the move," Mom says. "I'll have to think about it."

Two weeks before Mom and Paul got married, Mom and I moved out of our duplex, Paul moved out of his apartment, and the three of us moved into our house. We stayed in the same neighborhood, so it wasn't a huge change. Plus, we got a backyard.

"Could it be in the nursery closet?" I ask. The nursery has a walk-in closet where lots of things get shoved.

"No. I organized it before we put Boo's stuff in," Mom says.

"What about the basement? Or your closet?"

Mom sighs. "Do you need it right this instant?"

"I bet you know where Boo's baby book is right this instant," I mumble.

"What?"

"Nothing," I say.

When Ray made the baby foot and Priya made that comment about hospitals, it made me wonder if my baby book had my footprint in it. And *that* made me wonder if there were clues about my dad in there, too. But if Mom can't remember where the book is, my first official lead is a dead end.

I'm about to give up and walk away when Mom says, "You can try in the buffet. There's a lot of photo albums in there."

I tell her thanks and head to the dining room. The buffet belonged to my mom's mom. I don't remember her. She got cancer and died when I was three. My mom's dad died a year later. (I don't really remember him, either.) There are no dishes in the buffet, though. It's more like a giant junk drawer. Which works, since we don't use the dining room to eat anyway. It's Paul's puzzle room. That is, when it's not the storage place for boxes of diapers, totes of clothes, a high chair, and a playpen.

There are a few photo albums in the buffet, but no baby book. There are also stacks and stacks of loose photos. I grab a few handfuls and look through them. Some people I recognize (like me or my mom when we were younger), but most are strangers to me. On the back of the photos are random names and dates.

Uncle John and Aunt Milly. Calif. 1972
Cameron and Jessie, ages 11 & 9
For M—Love you. Don't ya forget!
Maui 2000

I shuffle through a few stacks before I get bored. Looking at pictures of people you don't know is like watching a movie in a different language with no subtitles.

When I go back to the living room, Mom is coming down the stairs.

"Here," she says, smiling and holding out my baby book. "I remembered where I put it."

"Thanks," I say.

"Need any help?"

"Nah. I'm good."

I take the book to my room, feeling hopeful. I've seen Boo's baby's book before. It has pages titled things like *All About Mommy* and *All About Daddy.* There was even a page called *All About Your Siblings.* I know because Paul interviewed me so he could fill it in. Mom and Paul put one of the sonogram photos they got in the book, too. They wrote *Your first picture!* under it. (The other sonogram is hanging on our refrigerator.)

I haven't seen my baby book since I was like five. It isn't as fancy. There's a section called *You're On Your Way* where Mom wrote a letter about how she found out she was pregnant and what her reaction was. *Excited and scared.* There's no mention of my dad in the letter.

I turn to the next page to see if there's one from him, but the pages skip ahead to things like Mom's baby shower and getting the nursery ready. I do find a series of three sonogram photos in the book, though. On the last one, someone electronically drew a circle around what I'm guessing are my legs. Along the edge, it says, *It's a boy!* I don't know how they could tell, though. It's dark and blurry. At least in the one of Boo on the refrigerator, you can kind of see her hand because it looks like she's waving.

Wasn't there a space for my dad to write a letter about how he found out and what his hopes and dreams were for me, too?

I inspect the book more closely and discover jagged edges in the book's gutter.

Holy cow. Someone tore out pages!

And by someone, I mean Mom. No one else would've done it. Did she rip them out after she and my dad broke up? Or maybe she did it because she knew I'd look someday. Either way, she had no right to do that.

I read through the rest of my baby book and the pictures and cards stuffed inside. I go through the plastic baggie with my and Mom's hospital wristbands, a few dried yellow roses, and a card with my newborn footprint. There are pictures of my first bath. My ride home. My first night at home. (Who took those?) My first step. My first word—*diggy,* which Mom wrote meant *doggy.* My first birthday. And all the way up to my tenth birthday.

But there is no sign of my dad. No photos with him. It's like he doesn't exist. Except I know he does, because *I* exist. Frustrated, I slam the book shut.

"Hey. Be careful with that," Mom says from my bedroom doorway.

"Sorry," I say, startled. How long has she been standing there?

She smiles. "Did you get what you needed?"

"Yes," I lie.

"Great. If you're done with it, can you please put it on my bed? I'll put it back in the cedar chest later."

The chest. Of course! I can't believe I didn't think of that.

Paul had a brother named Cole who was a couple of years older than him and some kind of master carpenter. He made this big chest when he was a senior in high school and won the grand prize ribbon at the state fair. Cole drowned at a lake party a week after he graduated, so Paul has had the chest ever since. He and Mom put it at the foot of their bed. They keep important and sentimental stuff in there, like souvenirs from their honeymoon. And Paul told Mom she could put her stuff from college in there after they ran out of space in the closet. I remember because it was a few days after we moved, and Paul joked about us already needing a bigger house.

If there's a good place to look for clues about my dad, Cole's chest would be it.

13

LOCARD AND HIS EXCHANGE PRINCIPLE

*The cedar chest might be the perfect place
for clues about my dad. But I'll need time to go
through it when Mom and Paul aren't around.*

For now, I need to concentrate on learning more investigation stuff. This way I'll be ready when I get the chance.

Mr. S clears his throat to get our attention and the Forensic Science Club settles down.

"We are honored to have Ms. Bunce here this afternoon to start off our week," he says. "Ms. Bunce is a trace evidence examiner and she'll be telling us about her fascinating job."

After thanking Mr. S for the introduction, Ms. Bunce casually leans against his desk.

"Tell me where you've been today," she says to a girl at the closest table.

The girl looks confused.

"There's no right or wrong answer. Just pick a place you visited today while at school."

"The cafeteria," the girl says.

"Perfect. What did you have for lunch?" Ms. Bunce asks.

"A sandwich, some chips, and a piece of cake my mom made."

"Did you leave anything?"

"At the cafeteria? I don't think so."

"What about your trash? Were there any cake crumbs?"

"Probably," the girl says.

Ms. Bunce points to Tomás. "Tell me someplace you went today."

"The football field. We had gym outside," he says.

"Do me a favor and check your shoes," Ms. Bunce says. "Are there tiny pieces of black rubber stuck on them? Or maybe on your socks?"

Tomás looks. "That would be an affirmative. How'd you know that?"

Ms. Bunce smiles. "Lucky guess. I used to be in marching band, and AstroTurf is notorious for leaving black bits on your shoes and socks. We called them Turf ticks."

Next, Ms. Bunce carefully pulls a long strand of hair off her shoulder and holds it up. "Whose hair is this? It might be mine—well, it probably is—but it might belong to the friend I hugged earlier. We don't know unless we test it.

"These are examples of trace evidence, the small but measurable things left at a crime scene," Ms. Bunce goes on. "Forensic science is based on the principle that every contact leaves a trace. This is known as Locard's exchange principle. Whenever we go someplace or touch something or someone, we're going to leave something behind. Or take something with us.

"My job is to look for that trace evidence and analyze it, see what it is and where, or who, it may have come from. Trace evidence is often the key to getting new leads for detectives, or even to solving the case."

Trace evidence examiner sounds like an interesting job. I wonder what my dad's job is. He probably has a regular kind of job. But for all I know, he could be famous. I heard about an actress who figured out her dad was a rock star because she realized she looked like him. I don't know of any famous short guys. None that I look like, anyway.

We spend the rest of our club time using microscopes to study slides of different kinds of hair and fibers. For the record, cat hair has scales on it that look like the bark of a palm tree.

After we finish, there are a few minutes left. Mr. S gives us a Five-Minute Mystery to solve. These are riddles or short mystery stories he introduces at the end of each club meeting. We don't play as a team, though. It's every person for themselves.

Mr. S shuffles his flash cards and then reads the one at the top of the deck. "Kathy can't go home because someone in a mask and someone with a bat are standing there. What should she do?"

Mr. S barely finishes reading before Casey stands up and heads to the front of the room to collect her Tootsie Roll Pop.

"Too easy!" she says, like it doesn't matter that Mr. S didn't even call on her. "It's a baseball game and Kathy should wait until the coach tells her to run home."

When we're dismissed, Casey and I end up walking out at the same time.

"That was the fastest Five-Minute Mystery solve ever," I say as we head down the hall toward the front doors. Since Ray has to stop and get his clarinet on the way out, his mom picks him up by the band room door on Mondays and Wednesdays.

Casey smiles. "My sister plays softball."

"That's cool."

"Yeah. She's kind of a big deal. She's been on TV for being the Athlete of the Week," Casey says. But it's not in a braggy kind of way. It's more like a sad way.

I'm not sure how to respond, so I say the first thing that comes into my head. "I used to play softball. I wasn't very good at it."

Casey laughs. "Yeah, my talents, like my pops tells me, lie elsewhere." She puts air quotes around the last two words.

"You seem good at forensic science so far," I say.

"You too, Shortlock."

We're quiet as we go through the doors and sit down on the Spirit Rock out in front of the school. The Spirit Rock is this giant rock that gets painted and repainted by different teams before games or the school council for holidays or events. We're not supposed to sit on it. Everyone does anyway.

Our rides aren't here yet, but we're not worried. There's a railroad crossing nearby where cars get stopped by trains a lot.

We sit in silence, but a few seconds later, Casey lets out a giant sigh.

"I really want to go to the tournament," she says. It takes me a second to realize she's talking about the interschool forensic science tournament.

I don't say anything. Like I said, Casey is like a balloon with too much air.

"My sister has a bunch of trophies from softball tournaments she's been to. They take up half of her room. It would be nice to know what it's like to have one. A trophy of my own, I mean. I have a room."

Her joke makes me smile.

"I want to be in the spotlight," she says. "Just for once, I want something to be about me. You know?"

"Yeah," I say. "I get that. I know what it's like to have a sibling everyone constantly talks about."

"Oh, right. Your mom is pregnant. Are she and your dad excited?"

"Stepdad," I correct her. "And yes, very."

"How long have you had a stepdad?" she asks. "Sorry. In addition to being gabby, I'm nosy. My dad says I should learn to mind my business and use my powers for good, not evil."

I laugh. "It's okay," I tell her. "Paul's been around for a couple of years."

"Do you know your dad?"

It's a simple enough question, but I stumble. "Uh . . . no," I finally answer.

Casey frowns. "That's too bad," she says.

I think about how Casey knows her bio-mom. And how much I'd like to know my dad, too. I'm surprised by what comes out of my mouth next.

"But I'm looking for him."

"For real?" Casey asks. "Like tracking down a missing person kind of thing?"

"Kind of," I tell her.

"What are you going to do when you find him?"

"Find a way to convince my mom to let me meet him," I say.

"Brilliant! I'll totally help," Casey says. I must give her a confused look, because she adds, "We can practice our forensic science skills. It'll be fun."

"Why would you do that?" I ask her.

"You're part of my team," Casey says, and shrugs. "Why not?"

It would be nice to have someone to talk to about trying to find my dad. It's not like I can talk to Mom. Or Ray.

A car honks. Casey's ride is here. She jumps off the rock and says, "So?"

Then she sticks out her hand.

And I shake it.

14

EARS AND EYES

Casey's got a list of ideas to help me find my dad.

"What about your birth certificate?" she asks before Forensic Science Club on Wednesday. I look around.

"Who are you looking for?" Casey asks.

"Ray and Priya."

"You want to wait for them?"

"Um...no. Can we..."

"Oh," Casey says. "This is a covert investigation. Got it. Okay. I'll be quick, then. Your birth certificate is where you should start."

I shake my head. "It's in a safe in my mom's closet."

"Can you get the combo?"

"I don't know where she keeps it. And if I ask her for it, she'll want to know why I need to get into the safe."

"You could break in?"

I give her a look.

"Okay. Okay. Do you have a baby book? I know my dads wrote *every* detail down in ours."

"Already looked. It wasn't any help. There's a chest that might have something, though," I tell her. "But it's in my mom's room, too, and I have to wait until I have time to look."

"All right. Keep me posted. What about your grandparents? Would they know anything about your dad?" Casey asks.

"They died when I was little."

"Oh. Sorry." Casey consults her list again. "Internet?" she says, and then taps her pencil against her chin before answering her own question. "Hmm. Never mind. That's probably not much help without a name. Unless your mom is famous or something."

Ray and Priya arrive together. "What are you two talking about?" Ray asks as the two of them sit down.

"The video," I say quickly, hoping Casey doesn't give anything away.

"What video?" Priya wants to know.

"You don't know? Felix and his mom are famous," Ray says. "His mom caught a foul ball about to hit him in the face and didn't even spill her drink."

"Wait," Casey says. "That was your mom? I think I saw that video."

"Me too!" Priya says.

"You and half of Ohio," I tell them. For the record, that's an exaggeration. Ohio has millions of people. I think the video got somewhere around fifty thousand views before it died down. But the story *did* make the local news, since Paul is hometown famous.

When the other two aren't looking, I mouth *Thank you* to Casey and she mouths *You're welcome* back.

"All righty, my favorite guinea pigs," Mr. S announces from the front of the room. "Your first crime is next Wednesday. There will be real, live witnesses to interview, and we need to be ready."

Mr. S displays an acronym up on the board:

Prepare for the interview and know what you want to ask ahead of time.

Let the witness tell their story, don't interrupt them.

Ask short, simple questions.

You—stay out of it! Don't lead or react.

Press for details.

Ears and eyes—pay attention to what they're saying and <u>how</u> they're saying it.

Notes—record the witness's response.

PLAYPEN. I should be able to remember that. I'll just think of Boo and how her stuff is taking over the house.

We go over each step.

"Letting the witness tell their story is one of the most challenging aspects of interviewing someone," Mr. S tells us. "We homo sapiens tend to like the sound of our own voices. But it's important to listen and then *wait*. Let the witness take their time in telling their story. Don't be tempted to speak because there's silence."

When we get to the Ears and Eyes part, Mr. S says, "This is another important skill to have when interviewing a person. Watch their body language. Watch their expressions. Listen to the tone of their voice."

Mr. S has a few volunteers come up to the front of the classroom. They each say the same phrase—"I like apples and bananas but not cantaloupe"—only he whispers in their ears ahead of time, telling them how to say it. Angry. Sad. Disappointed. Deceitful. Matter-of-fact. And we write down what we observe.

Afterward, we take turns interviewing members of our teams. Before long, everyone starts having *way* too much fun.

"Where were you on the night in question?"

"What was your reaction when you discovered the three corpses sitting around the kitchen table, appearing to play Monopoly?"

"So, tell me again about the streaker's sneakers."

Mr. S lets it slide for a while, but then reminds us, "Seven days, people."

My team interviews me about the viral video. I tell them about how I still have the batting helmet Paul brought me sitting on my dresser.

Casey is next. She tells us about the time she went to a birthday party and broke her wrist going down the inflatable water slide the birthday girl's parents rented. "My pops picked me up, took me to get a cast, and then I came back since it was a sleepover party," she says.

"What color was the cast?" Priya asks. (**P**—press for details.)

"Purple," Casey tells us.

We interview Priya about why she wants to be a medical examiner. She tells us that over the summer she and her friend came across a dead cat in the street.

"I thought it was fascinating," Priya says. "I wanted to know how it got there and what happened to it."

"What did your friend think?" I ask.

Priya frowns. "She thought it was gross." I remember Priya saying her friends think it's weird she wants to investigate dead bodies. It's hard to have your friends not understand something that's important to you. Like Ray doesn't understand me wanting to find my dad. Or probably wouldn't.

Ray's the last team member to go. Since we asked Priya about wanting to be a medical examiner, she asks him what he wants to be.

"A video game artist," he says.

"Why?" Casey asks.

I study Ray's body language and voice tone. (**E** for Ears and Eyes.)

"Because I'm good at art and I like video games," he says. "Duh."

"What your favorite game?" I ask. I already know, but he tells me anyway so we can record his answer.

"Is art your favorite subject?" Casey asks.

"Duh," Ray says again.

"Answer yes or no, please," Priya says. Man. She's serious about this interviewing stuff.

"Are you good at any other subjects?" Priya wants to know.

"Um. I'm good at history. And . . . uh. That's it."

There. Right there.

When Ray said, "That's it," his expression changed the tiniest bit. He looked down really quick and then back up.

Despite not wanting to be in Math Club, I know for a fact that Ray is in the advanced algebra class. And he's one of the top students.

I don't know if all father-and-son relationships are complicated. But I do know I'd like to find out for myself.

15

CRIME SCENE #1

Priya sharpened everyone's pencils and passed out notebooks ahead of time, so our team is ready to go the following Wednesday.

"Does everyone remember the plan?" she asks as we head to the cafeteria for our first crime scene. Since she plans on investigating for a living, she's our unofficial head detective.

Before we left the biology room, the four of us decided who was going to do what at the crime scene. Ray is in charge of sketching the scene. I'm going to take notes on the evidence. Casey is interviewing the witnesses-slash-possible-suspects. And Priya is going to walk around, taking in the big picture. Her job is to look for details Ray and I might miss, and to help Casey if she needs it. Priya will take the lead once we get back to the classroom.

When we get to the scene, Mr. S gives us an overview.

Our first crime is called the Case of the Sabotaged Cake. The high school forensic science class came over to set it up in the middle school's kitchen. Since it would be easy for evidence to get contaminated with five teams moving around, there's yellow caution tape that we have to stay behind. Everyone has twenty-five minutes to walk the perimeter, take notes, and interview suspects. *Most* of the evidence is marked.

"But here's the really fun part," Mr. S tells us. "There'll be two pieces of evidence that aren't marked, and they may help solve the case. If you spot something you think is an unmarked piece of evidence, go to the Evidence Expert"—here he points to a high schooler off to the side—"and ask if you're right. If you are, the expert will give you an envelope with more information about the evidence. The expert will also be available when we get back to the classroom in case you notice something later."

"We've totally got this," Casey whispers to the rest of the team. The four of us exchange fist bumps.

Mr. S then asks us to give our attention to the high schooler in charge.

"Every Wednesday, the cafeteria staff makes their famous chocolate cake," she says. "But yesterday, the cake was ruined when someone substituted powdered sugar for flour. Your job is to figure out who the saboteur is. Good luck!"

We spread out. I begin walking around and taking notes. I study the scene and try not to make any judgments. That's one of the things Ms. Bunce told us. "Remember to keep your eyes and your mind open," she said. "Observe, don't feel. Once we start thinking about how things *should* be, we lose track of how they *are*."

The high schoolers have set up place cards with letters to mark each piece of evidence. There's a small amount of powdery white substance on the floor (labeled item B), and a partial footprint (item E). I write down everything I see and describe it with as much detail as I can: the recipe card (item H), taped to a cabinet with a piece of masking tape; the opened box of vinyl gloves on an otherwise clear work counter (item C); the measuring cups, bowls, and spoons soaking in the sink; the office organizer on the counter where pens and tape are kept, with a pair of scissors lying nearby; the flat cake (item A); the open pantry door filled with clear plastic containers labeled FLOUR and POWDERED SUGAR (items J and K).

My team and I check in with each other a few times, and the twenty-five minutes goes by quickly. When we get back to Mr. S's room, he hands each team a case file with photographs, information about the evidence, and the suspects' fingerprints and shoe prints. Teams will get points for teamwork (one to three points), finding pieces of unmarked evidence (zero to two points), and the speed with which we solve the case (one to five points). There will be three crimes this fall, so three chances to earn points. The team with the most points gets to represent our school in the interschool tournament in December.

"Time starts now," Mr. S says, and the timer on the board begins counting down.

My team didn't find either of the unmarked clues while we were at the scene, but I think the three-person team found one. I saw Tomás go up to the Evidence Expert while we were in the cafeteria.

Priya takes out the photos of the scene and the suspects, the lab results, and the information in the case file and lays them out. The four of us study them carefully, following her first rule of science: Assess, then progress.

"Any fingerprints?" Ray asks.

Priya scans the information we have. "No prints."

"The person probably wore gloves," I say, pointing. "There's a box on the counter."

"What about this footprint?" Casey says, holding up the photo of a partial footprint in what appears to be flour on the kitchen floor. "Looks like a tennis shoe." On Monday, we learned about footprints and shoe and tire tread marks.

Ray nods. "Let's check the suspects' shoes and see if there's a possible match."

Priya locates the photos of our three suspects. (Played by high schoolers.) They're each wearing hairnets and aprons, which are covered with powdery white handprints. All three have on tennis shoes.

"Where're the shoe prints?" Casey asks, searching through the file photos. "Here."

The four of us compare the print in the powder to the shoe prints the suspects provided.

"Well, that doesn't help much," Ray says when we determine there isn't an exact match.

"I think we can at least rule out the short cook, though," Casey says. "Look at her feet. Her shoes must be too small for this print."

"I dunno," I say, drawing it out. "You can't always trust short people. They're low-down."

It takes my team a few seconds to get the joke. When they do, Ray and Priya groan, and Casey slugs me playfully. "Low-down," she says. "Good one."

Priya has Casey read out her notes from interviewing the witnesses. But nothing seems unusual.

Anticipation runs through the room like an electrical current. Tomás's team is talking excitedly at the table closest to us. It's hard not to hear snippets of everyone's conversations and wonder if they're onto something. But you can't listen too intently or look over for long. Mr. S told us any form of cheating would result in the whole team being disqualified for that crime.

The four of us go back to the photos and Ray's sketches.

"Hmmm...What aren't we seeing?" Priya says, more to herself than to us.

"Are you sure you got notes on all the evidence?" Ray asks me.

"Yes. Are you sure you sketched everything?" I say, annoyed.

Casey puts her hand up. "Stop. We're getting nowhere. We need to gather our Zen."

"Gather our what?" Ray asks.

"Our Zen. It means let's take a deep breath. I learned it in yoga."

"You do yoga?" Ray asks her.

"You don't?" Casey counters.

"Come on," Priya says. "We don't have time for this. We have to focus."

"Trust me," Casey says. "It'll *help* our focus. Ten seconds. That's all it'll take."

It's easier (and frankly, faster) to agree than argue, so Ray, Priya, and I follow Casey's instructions. She inhales deeply and slowly lets it out, using her fingers to count to five and then back down to one.

Casey was right. I feel more focused. I bet Ray does, too, though he'd probably never admit it.

We go back to comparing photos and sketches and reading evidence notes, going over each section of the crime scene, one by one this time.

Ray sits back and closes his eyes.

"What are you doing?" Casey asks. "This is no time for a nap."

Ray keeps his eyes closed. "I'm visualizing the scene, running through everything in my head again," he says. "Shh. It helps me."

The three of us give a collective shrug and go on without him.

"Wait!" Ray says a few minutes later. He grabs his sketch and then the photo of the scene.

"Look. There's something on that one suspect's shoe. What if it's powdered sugar? That would be a dead giveaway."

The rest of my team leans in closer to inspect it. "You're right!" Priya tells him. "That might be one of the unmarked pieces of evidence."

Priya and Casey walk over to the Evidence Expert and ask if we're right. The girl hands them an envelope.

"Yes," Ray says, and pumps his hand when they return. Priya tears open the envelope and reads the test results.

"'Testing done on the substance on suspect number three's left tennis shoe indicated substance is: all-purpose flour.'"

My team groans in unison.

"What did the suspects say again?" I ask Casey.

She gives us another rundown. "Suspect number one has been a cook at the middle school for two years. She claims she was helping unload the supply truck the whole time.

"Suspect number two is the head baker. She says she was sure she didn't mix up the two ingredients because she'd used the last of the powdered sugar the day before and she hadn't put more in the container yet.

"Suspect number three is brand-new. She said she wasn't even near the cake bowl because she was busy chopping vegetables."

Ray rummages through files. "The security camera footage backs up suspect number one's story. It wasn't her."

Something is niggling at my brain. It's like when you wake up from a dream and you can't quite remember it, but you know it was good.

I go over Ray's sketch and the photos one more time. Something catches my attention.

Actually, two somethings.

16

SHORTLOCK HOLMES DOES IT AGAIN

"Look at the pantry," I say, pointing. "There's powdered sugar in the powdered sugar container."

"Yeah . . . ?" Ray sounds confused.

"The head baker said she'd used the last of it the day before and hadn't replaced it yet. Why is it mostly full?"

"Someone must have opened a new bag," Casey says.

"Or the head baker lied," Ray offers.

"That's possible," Priya says.

"Okay. But assuming the head baker didn't lie," Casey says, "how does someone opening a new bag help us?"

"The scissors," I whisper so the other teams can't hear. "Someone used scissors to open the new bag. See? They didn't put them away." I point to the crime scene photo showing the counter.

"But they were wearing gloves, remember?" Ray asks. "There aren't any prints at the scene."

"Maybe they were careless and did that first, before they put on gloves," I say. "It's worth a shot."

Without saying anything else, I walk up to the Evidence Expert and give her my answer for the second unmarked clue. She smiles and hands me an envelope.

Yes!

My hands shake as I open the new information. "'Single fingerprint found on the scissors. Photo attached.'"

The four of us compare the fingerprint lifted from the handle of the scissors to the fingerprints of the three suspects. There's a clear match: suspect number three. The new girl.

My team and I hurry to the front of the room and present our evidence and conclusion. Mr. S stands up from behind his desk. "Attention, everyone. We have our first correct summation of the evidence."

Casey high-fives me on our way back to the table. "Shortlock Holmes does it again," she says.

Mom and I stopped at the grocery store on the way home to get the ingredients for my favorite dinner to celebrate. I'm helping her put stuff away and telling her about the crime when Paul comes in.

"Oh, let me get that," Paul says, reaching for the gallon of milk in Mom's hand. "You need to take it easy."

Mom shoos him away. "If I can grow a human, I can carry milk," she says.

I laugh. Paul does, too, and then he throws up his hands in defeat before leaving the kitchen.

"We got this, right?" Mom asks me.

"Yep."

And we do. We've had a good system for forever. There was never anyone to watch me, so I had to go shopping with Mom. She bribed me with candy and called us the Dynamic Duo.

Things would have been different if my dad had been around. I don't mean better—Mom and I made a great team. But maybe my dad and I would have been our own Dynamic Duo. After today's win, and with Casey's help, I know I can find him. I just need one good lead to get me started.

"Man," Mom says, interrupting my thoughts. "I lived on these when I was in college." She waves a box of toaster pastries.

Since we're finished with the groceries, the two of us sit down at the kitchen table. "Wanna split one before dinner?" Mom asks like she's the kid instead of the grown-up. "I don't know about you, but I'm starving."

"Me too," I tell her. We split the package and eat our pastries without even warming them up in the toaster.

"My roommate thought it was gross I ate these straight out of the box," Mom tells me.

I know where Mom went to college, but she doesn't talk about it much. I figure that's because I came along and interrupted her junior year and then she and my dad went their separate ways. This time, she's the one who brought it up.

Here's my chance to ask more. And maybe get a clue about my dad.

What was it we learned in Forensic Science Club last week? Oh, yeah. PLAYPEN. I start with A—Ask short, simple questions.

"How did your roommate like to eat them?"

I try to keep my face neutral; that's what Mr. S told us to do. (*Stay out of it. Don't lead the witness or react to what they're saying,* he said.)

"Kelly?" Mom responds. "Oh, she preferred them frozen. She kept a box stuffed in our dorm's fridge."

"You're allowed to have refrigerators in your rooms when

you're in college?" I ask, completely forgetting the *Don't react* rule.

Mom grabs the pastry wrapper before standing up. "Yep. Mini ones, anyway. You couldn't have a toaster, though. There was one down the hall in the common kitchen, but I was lazy. I guess that's why I ended up eating these right out of the box."

"Did you like living in the dorm?"

"Loved it. My friends were there," Mom tells me. She throws away the wrapper and grabs a knife and cutting board to chop an onion for the chili.

"What kind of things did you and your friends do?" I ask.

Mom stops what she's doing and looks at me. I can't tell if she's trying to remember what she did or wondering why I'm suddenly interested in her college days. *Am I being too obvious?* I wonder. Finally, she starts talking again.

"Oh, lots of things," she says, turning her attention back to the onion. "I tailgated for football games, went to see plays. And once a week, I'd volunteer at the animal shelter. We'd take the dogs out for walks."

"Hold on," I say. "You walked dogs in college but won't let *me* get one? I thought you didn't like them."

Mom laughs. And I realize I've broken the rule about not reacting again.

"Maybe when Boo is old enough, we'll get one," she says. "I like dogs, Felix. There are a lot of things you don't know about me. Believe it or not, I was the quarterback on a flag football team!"

"Really?"

"Really," she says. "It was an intermural team, of course. And it was coed."

I cock my eyebrow, and Mom laughs again.

"Unlike middle school dances, boys and girls hang out all the time in college," Mom says. "And even though it might not look like it in my current state"—she motions to her round Boo belly—"I was a decent athlete."

I haven't been to a middle school dance yet. But I know a bit about football.

"You? Quarterback?" I ask.

"I have a photograph somewhere," Mom says. "I'll dig it up for you sometime."

"Who was on your team?"

"Well, let me think," Mom says, moving on to chopping a clove of garlic. "There were ten of us. Kelly was on it. And Kate. She lived across the hall from me and Kelly. Kelly's boyfriend, Steve. Debbie."

Mom starts ticking names off with her other hand. I watch her body language and listen closely.

"Hudson, Dave, Cynthia . . . How many is that? Two more. Oh, right, Carter, he was roommates with Mikey."

She hesitates before saying this last name. Just for the tiniest bit, but I notice. Like Ray did when he lied about not being good at any subject besides art and history.

Mom slides the onion and garlic into the pot and then turns to me. "Okay, mister. Stop interrogating and let me get back to fixing dinner," she teases. "I'm sure you have some homework you could be doing, too," she adds as if it isn't already clear our conversation is over.

I drag out my backpack and try to focus on my assignment. But it's not math I'm thinking about. It's me.

My middle name is Michael.

17

HUGE NEWS

I thought I got my middle name because my mom heard it somewhere and liked it. But Michael must be my dad's name, based on Mom's reaction yesterday. It's got to be.

I can't talk to Casey with Ray sitting next to me in our bus seat. I text her instead.

Hey. Is your phone on?
Yes. Obviously lol.
I need to talk to you about our investigation. Come find me.

After we get to school and climb off the bus, I stop to tie my shoe and tell Ray to go on without me. Casey finds me a few seconds later and I replay the whole conversation I had with my mom.

"You're right," she says with the same confidence I feel. "That's your dad's name for sure. Now what?"

"I tried going online and searching *Michael* and the college name. Then I tried searching for my mom's name and *Michael*. I even searched for pictures of intermural flag football teams. But everything was a bust," I say.

Casey frowns. "Yeah. I can imagine. Still, this is huge."

"It feels huge."

Casey snaps her fingers. "Do you know any of your mom's college friends? I mean, does she talk to them and stuff? They might know something."

"Not that I know of. But we're going to a baby shower this weekend," I tell her. "Maybe I could do a bit of investigating."

"That sounds perfect, Shortlock!" Casey says.

Even though I'm hoping to find someone who knew Mom back in college, I'm not thrilled about the baby shower. I pull on the neck of my shirt as we arrive at the house of one of Mom's friends on Sunday.

"The shots must be working," Mom says. "You're outgrowing your clothes."

She looks excited, so I don't tell her that no, the shirt is just uncomfortable.

The inside of the house looks like someone threw up Easter. There's pink and green and yellow everywhere. But mostly pink. Don't people know that babies can wear any color, no matter if they're a boy or a girl?

"The family of the hour is here!" the host announces.

Everyone oohs and ahhs and comes over to touch Mom's belly and shake Paul's hand. A few people shake my hand, too. I focus on listening to Mom and Paul talk to see if I can pick up on any clues about college friends. But they all seem like work or neighborhood friends.

As Mom and Paul blend into the sea of adults, I try to dig deeper. Someone here must have known my mom when she went to college. Right?

"It's nice to meet you, too," I tell a woman who stops me. "How do you know my mom?"

"Have you been friends with my mom for a long time?" I ask someone else.

"What's the score?" I ask a man who's pulled up a college football game on his phone. "My mom went to that school. Did you go there, too?"

But I get nothing.

I'm leaning against a wall near the piano in the living room when Mom sneaks over and nudges me. "You don't need to hang around with us boring adults," she says. "Why don't you go get some food in the kitchen." And I take a break.

Boo's due in eight weeks. Ish. Her dad will be there when she's born. She'll never know what it's like to not have him around. But if I want to have my dad around—ever—I need to find him fast. Once Mom and Paul change their last names in January, my dad won't be able to find *me*.

If he wants to, that is.

There are a couple of younger kids at a card table in the corner of the dining room. They're busy playing with Play-Doh and coloring.

"How old are you?" one of the kids asks me as I walk past them with my plate of food.

"Eleven," I tell him.

He stops rolling the clay snake he's making. "No way."

"Way," I say annoyed. Grown-ups or people my age thinking I'm younger than I am is okay, but I hate when little kids do it.

"I'm eight and I'm bigger than you," the kid says.

"So."

"I bet I could beat you up."

"No you couldn't," I say. Before he can argue, I walk back to the kitchen to get another cup of punch. On my way, a man and a woman stop me.

"Felix! It's nice to see you again. How are you?" the woman says.

It takes me a second to remember who they are because I wasn't expecting them to be here. They're Paul's mom and dad, who live in Indiana.

"Nice to see you again, too—"

They've told me I can call them Tom and Janna, or even Grandma and Grandpa if I'd like. But neither feels right. Mostly, I avoid calling them anything.

Tom explains that they drove in last-minute to surprise Mom and Paul. "Unfortunately, we're driving home right after the party," he tells me.

"But we'll be back after the baby comes, of course!" Janna adds.

Janna asks me about school, and I tell her about Forensic Science Club. "It's a lot of fun," I tell them. "My team was first to solve our first crime this week."

"Congratulations," Tom says.

"Oh! I can't wait to be a grandma," Janna bursts out, clasping her hands to her chest. "Babies are such a blessing! I'm looking forward to dressing her up in tiny clothes and baby shoes."

Tom gives me a wink. "You'll have to excuse her. She's been waiting a long time. We both have."

I look at Tom and Janna, beaming and acting gaga. Boo's going to call them Grandma and Grandpa, but they'll probably always be Tom and Janna to me.

Later on, everyone plays a bunch of games. Mom and Paul insist that I join in. I don't mind; I kill it in the Guess the Melted Candy Bar in the Diaper game. The secret is smelling it. Mr. S says, when examining evidence, we need to use all of our senses.

Next, it's time for cake and presents.

There's a mountain of boxes. Mom unwraps tons of diapers and pink booties and socks and dresses that look like they belong on a doll. Someone gives her a miniature tea set made out of real china. Which is stupid if you ask me, but no one does.

The "big" present is from Tom and Janna. It's a fancy stroller.

Man. Boo's not even born and she's cleaning up. Mom and Paul will probably have to pile stuff on top of me in the backseat for us to get home in one trip.

There's even another present *inside* the stroller.

"This one is for you, Felix," Mom says, pulling it out.

Me?

I squish between Mom and Paul on the couch to open it.

"That's from us," Janna says.

"Thank you," I tell her.

It's one of those clear storage boxes. On the top, someone has painted *Big Brother Survival Kit*. Inside the box there's a pair of earplugs (these get a laugh from the rest of the room), a bunch of bags of chips and granola bars, a video game, a cloth diaper ("To protect your shoulder from spit-up," Janna explains. More laughs), and a T-shirt that says: ~~ONLY CHILD~~ BIG BROTHER.

At the end of the party, Janna and Tom come over to say goodbye.

"Thanks again for the present," I tell them. "I wasn't expecting that."

Tom smiles. "It was our pleasure," he says.

After that, Mom and Paul spend forty-five minutes saying goodbye to the party guests. Thankfully we're able to make it home in one trip. I have to share the backseat with presents, but at least they aren't suffocating me.

Paul and I start unloading the car in the driveway while Mom grabs the mail. She comes waddling over as fast as she can with a big grin on her face.

"Look," she says, waving an opened letter. "There was a cancellation and our court date got moved up! We're scheduled for November twenty-third. The Monday before Thanksgiving. Isn't that great news?"

18

BREAKING AND ENTERING

Thirty days.

That's how long until Mom and Paul go to court to change their last names. I counted this morning.

"I have two months less than I thought I had to find my dad," I tell Casey on the bus Monday. (Ray's not riding today because he has an early dentist appointment.)

"What do you mean?" she asks.

I explain how my mom and Paul are changing their last names and it was supposed to be in January, but now it's not. And once it happens, my dad wouldn't be able to find me online.

"What about the viral video? Wouldn't it show up if he searched for your mom online?"

"Our names aren't in the video."

She shrugs. "Maybe he'll see the video and recognize her."

"The video is old news now. Besides, my mom was wearing a big hat and sunglasses," I explain. "Some of her friends didn't even recognize her. I can't take that chance."

"You've got a point," Casey admits. "But you still have time to find *him*. Don't give up now. I know we can do it."

"How?"

"Have you looked in that chest you told me about?" she asks.

"Not yet," I tell her. "But I have a plan."

Later that night, I put my plan into motion when Paul and I are alone.

"You know what?" I say. "Mom fell asleep on the couch. You should go get some ice cream before she wakes up."

"Is Jeni's open this late?" Paul asks.

"Yes. I just checked."

Paul holds out his fist for a bump. "You're a good son. You know that?"

The good son part makes me feel guilty. But I don't have a choice. I need to get into the chest.

After Paul leaves, I grab a roll of clear packing tape, a blank note card, and cocoa powder in case I find any fingerprints. Then I check on Mom one more time to make sure she's asleep. I lay a blanket over her to keep her warm. Hopefully, that'll help her stay asleep, too.

I'm sweating as I sneak into Mom and Paul's bedroom like I'm a burglar. I texted Casey for some moral support as soon as Paul left, but she hasn't responded.

Here it is. Cole's cedar chest.

I haven't looked at it up close before. It's a simple box.

Maybe five feet wide, a couple of feet tall, and a couple of fe
from front to back. I run my hand along the dark wood ar
wonder what Paul's brother was like. Did he and Paul loc
alike? Did they hang out? I wonder if Boo and I will hang ou
together. Probably not, since she'll be eleven years younger
I'll be starting high school when she starts preschool.

Focus, I tell myself.

I reach for the lid and lift. It doesn't budge. Cole was such
a good carpenter, he even built a lock. The keyhole is in the
middle of a smallish, raised square block of wood.

Great. Now what?

I search Mom's jewelry box and don't find the key. It's not
in Paul's valet box on top of the dresser, either. It might be
inside one of their drawers, but there's no way I can go through
their clothes and underwear. (1) Gross. And (2) They'd notice.

Still no response from Casey. I'm on my own as I consider
the pros and cons of breaking into the chest.

Pros:

**The chest is the most likely place Mom would
keep information about my dad.**

**It looks like a simple lock; I bet I could pick it no
problem.**

Cons:

Mom could wake up any minute.

**Paul will be home soon. Also, he could decide to
try the grocery store instead of the ice cream shop,
since the store sells Jeni's brand.**

I don't know how to pick a lock; I've only seen people do it on TV.

I could be wrong about the chest having any clues.

I stare at the chest, hoping it magically unlocked while I was debating. No such luck. It's decision time.

There's a pocketknife in Paul's valet box. I go to grab it and hear a creak downstairs. My breath catches as I stop to listen for Mom.

Silence.

I get the knife and then sit back down in front of the chest. *Am I really going to do this?*

You don't have a choice, a voice in my head says. *Thirty days.*

I wiggle the tip of the knife inside the lock. It feels like it's hit something. I press harder and twist the knife. I must twist too hard because, suddenly, something gives.

Crack.

The block of wood with the keyhole spins freely.

The keyhole was a decoy. The lock was a simple puzzle. You just had to turn the square block counterclockwise.

Oh, no.

I try to turn the block back into place. But it keeps swinging down so that the keyhole is upside down. I notice there's a gouge from the knife on the lid, too, from when my hand slipped.

My heart drops into my stomach. The chest is open, and I'm running out of time. Quickly but carefully, I begin pulling things out, searching for clues to who my dad is and where he might be.

I find what I'm looking for at the bottom of the chest.

19

JACKPOT

*It's a flat box, the kind you might gift-wrap a
sweater in, and it's labeled with the name of Mom's
college. Inside, there's a handful of mementos,
including a movie ticket stub that's from the year
before I was born and some dried yellow roses.
I'm guessing a boyfriend-girlfriend thing.*

I pull the box out and set it on the floor in front of me. There's
more.

An empty bag of M&M's.
A crossword puzzle book.
A CD.
A photograph.
And a T-shirt.

I'm not sure what's with the candy bag. My mom likes
M&M's just fine, but maybe it's an inside joke. Her name is
Marcy. And if my dad's name really is Michael, that could
make sense. Mikey plus Marcy. M&M.

I move on to the book. This one I get. My mom loves crossword puzzles. We do them as a family at dinner sometimes. I thumb through the book; all the puzzles are finished. (In ink, too, because Mom insists that's the only proper way to do them.) On the inside cover, there's an inscription written with a thin blue felt-tip marker. It's definitely not my mom's handwriting.

To M—
Clue: a four-letter word for how I feel about you that starts with L. Don't ya forget!

There's no signature, only a stick figure with an oversize smiley face holding a tiny heart. I roll my eyes. It's as cheesy as Paul and his "favorite girls" thing.

I glance at my phone to see how long Paul has been gone. (Fifteen minutes.) There's a text from Casey: Good luck. Remember to take pictures of anything you find.

Straining my ears, I hear nothing from downstairs except for the quiet drone of whatever television show Mom fell asleep watching.

I move on to the rest of the box. The CD is one of those mix things I've heard about where someone records a bunch of songs from different singers or music groups onto one CD. Mom says they're what people used for playlists before streaming services. The CD case has a cover with a picture of a movie theater marquee. The top of the marquee says ATH-ENA. One of the movie titles matches the ticket stub I found. My mom and dad must have gone on a date there. The picture was printed on a regular piece of paper (instead of shiny photo paper) so it's not very bright. When I open the case, the inside cover has a list of songs, printed from a computer. I don't recognize most of them, or the artists. I take a picture of the case and the song list. While I'm at it, I take pictures of the empty candy wrapper and the crossword book, too.

The CD itself is blank, no writing on it. I take it out to examine the other side, careful to hold it by the edges.

Whoa. There's a fingerprint on the shiny silver surface!

I pull out the supplies I brought, but shoot! I forgot a brush to dust the cocoa powder. There's a makeup brush on Mom's bathroom counter that'll have to do.

My hands shake but I manage to lift the fingerprint off the CD and tape it to the note card. There's no time to study it. After a hurried photograph, I shove the note card into the front pocket of my hoodie. I do my best to blow the rest of the cocoa powder off Mom's makeup brush and put it back where I found it.

Paul's been gone for twenty-three minutes now. He's bound to be home any second.

The photograph sits on top of the T-shirt. It's a five-by-seven print of a group of ten people. An equal mix of boys and girls. One of the girls is my mom. She looks way younger but it's definitely her, and she has her arms around the two girls next to her. There's a football on the grass in front of the group and everyone is smiling and wearing a short-sleeved lime-green T-shirt that says RABID SQUIRRELS. This must be the photograph Mom was talking about, the one of her college flag football team. That means one of these guys must be Mikey.

My dad.

I study each guy's face and look at their eye and hair color. It's hard to tell how tall everyone is because they're sitting or kneeling on the field, bunched together. Any of them could be my dad.

The last thing in the box is an actual Rabid Squirrels T-shirt. It has a tear along the right sleeve seam. I bring the shirt up to my nose because Ms. Bunce, the guest speaker at Forensic Science Club, said odor can be trace evidence. But it smells like the cedar wood that lines the chest.

Even though it doesn't smell used, the shirt sure looks used. I hold it up to inspect it closer. Besides the tear in the sleeve, there are what appear to be mud and grass stains. (Mr. S says we should never assume things about evidence.) I guess even though it was a flag football league, people hit the field a lot.

Turning it over, I find more stains. And a last name. But it's not Fine, like I expected. This isn't my mom's shirt.

Wilson.

My dad's last name is Wilson.

My nerves are buzzing so badly that when my phone vibrates, I literally jump.

Casey: How's it going?

I don't have time to answer her. Instead, I take a picture of the photograph and then put everything back in the box. Well, almost everything. I load the rest of the items back in the chest, just the way I found them.

The broken lock and the gouge on the lid make me want to shrink up and disappear. I pull down the corner of one of the blankets on top of the chest to hide them. How is Paul going to feel when he sees what I've done? The best I can hope for is that he doesn't notice.

As it turns out, there isn't time for anything other than hope. The garage door is opening.

20

WHITE LIE #1

*I run to my room and hide the Rabid Squirrels
T-shirt in the back of my closet. I'm not sure why
I took it, really. I like the team name; it's funny.
But I think I just wanted something of my dad's.
Hopefully, Mom won't miss it.*

Paul is clanging around in the kitchen and Mom is awake when I come downstairs.

"I was doing homework," I say, even though no one asks.

"What's this?" Mom wants to know when Paul walks in carrying a tray with three bowls of ice cream and spoons.

"*This* is your favorite ice cream," Paul tells her. "A post-nap snack."

"Wow. How sweet," Mom says.

"I'd love to take full credit," Paul says. "But it was Felix's idea. I was the carryout man."

Mom and Paul are smiling in my direction. But all I feel is guilt. The lock on the chest Cole made is broken. And there's a deep scratch on the lid. Both thanks to me. How can I sit and pretend everything is fine?

And how long before someone notices the damage?

I'm being text-bombed by Casey, so after I finish my bowl of ice cream, I excuse myself to my room.

What did you find?! she wants to know. I fill her in and forward the pictures I took. I don't tell her about what I did to Cole's chest, though.

Casey and I text back and forth as we investigate. She does a reverse-image search on the picture of the movie marquee. It's from a historic theater in the town where my mom and dad went to college. It opened in 1915, Casey texts. It's one of the oldest in the nation.

Not wanting to hurt her feelings, I text back Interesting but relevance?

While she's reading about the Athena theater, I search the internet with my dad's name. There are pages and pages of Michael Wilsons.

Try adding the college name, Casey suggests.

This time I find my dad's name listed along with his graduation year and major: civil engineering. Casey tells me it means he helps plan cities and roadways and stuff like that.

Is this a fingerprint? Casey texts, attaching the photo of the note card. I tried enlarging but it's not super clear.

I text back. Hold on . . .

I go to take a clearer shot and discover the note card isn't in my sweatshirt pocket anymore. Oh, man. I hope it didn't fall out in Mom and Paul's bedroom.

Can't find it. Will send another picture later.

Casey sends a thumbs-up emoji.

I tell her it's time to get my shot and that I'll see her tomorrow.

Casey wastes no time replying.

What kind of shot?! What's it for?

Shoot. Why did I write that? I debate for a minute or two whether to tell Casey anything. But then I figure, why not? She knows about me searching for my dad. She might as well know about the growth hormone deficiency, too.

That's cool, she texts when I'm done explaining it.

I don't want anyone else to know right now, I text back. There are three flashing dots on my phone screen. I'm preparing for Casey to argue, saying how it's not a big deal and why don't I want anyone to know and no one will care. But in the end, her response is short and sweet.

Also cool. I got your back.

"Oh, hey," Mom says when we're sitting down to dinner on Thursday. "I've been meaning to give this to you. I found it a few days ago. I'm assuming it's yours."

She's holding the note card with the fingerprint. I nod, my whole mouth suddenly too dry to speak. I've been looking for it everywhere.

"Is it for Forensic Science Club? Or have we been burglarized by a person kind enough to leave his or her fingerprint behind?" Mom asks playfully. "I found it in the front hall closet when I went to get the vacuum. It must have been kicked under the door."

Now that I know she didn't find it in her bedroom, I find my voice. "Yeah. It's for forensics. It's homework. We're supposed to compare them to other prints we find at home."

Homework? What kind of club has homework? Ugh.

It's just a little white lie. All I could come up with on the spot. But Mom buys it.

"That sounds like fun," she says. "Ooo. I know. After dinner, Paul and I can give you our prints, too. I've always wanted to be fingerprinted. Guess I have a mysterious criminal side."

I don't know about Mom, but I'm definitely feeling like I have a criminal side. I shouldn't have broken into the chest. At the very least, I should've been more careful with it.

Like she suggested, I set up a fingerprinting station after dinner and lift Mom's and Paul's fingerprints from glasses. I use ink instead of cocoa powder this time, though.

Paul watches closely. "This is interesting stuff," he says. "I'm bummed they didn't have clubs like this when I was in middle school. Who knows? I could've been a detective and not a news reporter."

"And then we would've never met," Mom tells him. The two of them exchange embarrassing googly eyes.

"There's going to be a special crime scene for parents at the tournament," I tell Paul.

"Really?" he asks excitedly.

"Yeah, Mr. S told us about it yesterday. Since parents won't be allowed to watch the teams while they work, the organizers decided to give them something to do while they wait. Correct answers will be entered in a drawing for gift certificates. If my team goes to the tournament, you could come do that," I tell him.

Paul grins. "Who cares about gift certificates? That would be awesome on its own. When will you find out if you're going?"

"We have two more crime scenes," I tell him. "Then we'll know."

"Sweet!"

It's funny to hear Paul using slang and I laugh. "Less laughing. More practicing," he teases.

I go to make my fingerprint on a glass, and Mom says, "I thought the one on the card was yours."

"Uh. It's not as clear as an ink one would be," I tell her, and then shove the note card with the CD fingerprint into my pocket. I'm getting good at this lying-on-the-spot thing. Which doesn't make me happy. But sharing what I learned in Forensic Science Club does.

I lift my print and tell Mom and Paul about the different patterns prints can have. "See? Mine is called a tented arch. It's the least common."

Mom has a whorl pattern, the one that reminds me of a universe.

"Hey, look," Paul says. "Mine looks like yours, Felix. Neat, huh?"

"Yeah," I say. "It is." I'm surprised that Paul and I have a similar pattern. What are the odds that my dad and I will have a similar fingerprint, too? Probably not great.

Later, alone in my room, I pull out the note card and compare the print to the one I made earlier. The one from the CD is smudged because I used cocoa powder instead of ink, but it's clear enough to see.

The patterns aren't similar.

Mr. S would tell me that I need to rule out other suspects, so I compare the print I took from the CD with Mom and Paul's fingerprints, too.

Clear match: Mom.

The only thing I have that belonged to my dad is an old T-shirt. How is that going to help me find him?

21
BRAXTON WHO?

It's Sunday. Paul, Mom, and I are decorating the front yard for Halloween. Well, Mom's supervising because she can hardly bend over anymore.

Paul and I have already planted a dozen tombstones with funny things written on them, like TOMB SWEET TOMB and REST IN PIECES. (My favorite is IMA GONER.) And now we're shoving sections of metal garden fencing into the ground in front of the fake cemetery to keep trick-or-treaters from running through it.

"*Ahhh,*" Paul says. "There's nothing like a creepy fence to add ambience," he says.

Mom shakes her head good-naturedly.

"What do you think, Felix?" Paul asks. I stand back and take it in. Last year, Paul went crazy and bought a bunch of decorations. He said it was because he'd lived in an apartment and never got to decorate anything besides his front door.

"I think we need more bones poking out of the ground," I conclude.

"See?" Paul says. "The kid knows what I'm talking about."

Mom laughs. "You guys are cut from the same cloth."

"I prefer to think of us as two bats from the same cave," Paul says.

I like that Paul is into the spooky stuff. When it was just me and Mom, we'd carve a pumpkin but that was about it. I probably got my love of scary things from my dad.

Mom tells me and Paul that she's going in to make hot chocolate. We start stringing strands of purple and orange miniature lights along the fence in front of the fake cemetery.

After a bit, we notice Mom hasn't come back out with the drinks. Paul goes to investigate while I grab the empty light boxes to throw into the recycling bin. When I get to the kitchen, Mom is leaning against the counter, gripping the edge with one hand. Paul's holding her other hand.

"What is it?" Paul asks.

"It's nothing," Mom says. She looks from me to Paul. "Really. Don't look so panicked, you two."

"It's not nothing," Paul says. "Is it the baby?"

Mom straightens herself up. "Don't worry. It's Braxton Hicks. Completely normal. I promise."

"Who's Braxton Hicks?" I ask.

Mom gives me a smile. "Not who, what. Braxton Hicks are like practice contractions. I got them all the time with you." Then she turns to Paul. "They're very common at this stage of pregnancy. Remember the birth instructor talking about them? And the dozens of books you've read?"

She's teasing him. But Paul's not having it. "Should we call the doctor?" he asks.

"No," Mom tells him. "Stop worrying. They'll go away soon."

"What if they don't?" Paul asks.

"If they don't stop, *then* we can call," Mom tells him. "But seriously. It's okay."

"I'm going to reread what the books say," he tells her.

"Be my guest," Mom says. "There'll be a quiz later." She's still teasing and this time, Paul relaxes a bit.

He insists on making dinner so Mom can rest. The whole time we're eating, Paul keeps looking over at Mom like something is about to happen and he's ready to spring into action. But like Mom said they would, the practice contractions went away.

I can tell Paul is relieved. I am, too.

It's weird. I know Boo is coming. I've seen the ultrasound pictures and watched my mom's stomach jump when my sister has gotten the hiccups. But before tonight, I didn't think about Boo *really* coming. There's going to be an actual baby living in our house.

In less than two months, it'll be Babysville around here. Crying around the clock. Cranky, sleep-deprived adults. Smelly diapers. Burping and barfing and baby talk. Onesies and tiny pink outfits in the laundry basket, baby toys everywhere. The rabbit lamp officially won't be mine anymore. And Mom and Paul won't have a lot of time for me.

That's another reason finding my dad is important. Maybe I could hang out with him when Mom and Paul are busy. Mom would tell me I'm being silly, that that's not how families work and that love isn't a pie divided up into pieces. But I know the truth. Once my sister comes, everything is going to change.

22

WHITE LIE #2

Casey has another idea for a lead, so I meet her by the Spirit Rock after Forensic Science Club the next day.

"What's up?" I ask.

Casey climbs on the rock and stands up like she's queen and the parking lot is her country. "You should call their college," she announces triumphantly.

"How would that help? He doesn't go there anymore," I reply.

"If you call the alumni department, they can tell you where he lives," Casey answers.

"They can?"

"My sister is applying to colleges. Remember? She has interviews with alumni who live in town. Pretend you're applying or something."

"No offense, but that's a dumb idea. They'll know I'm lying when they hear my voice."

"No one cares or can even tell how old someone is over the phone. And it's not like you have to give them your name or anything," Casey argues.

"I don't know. What about privacy laws and stuff?"

Casey lifts and drops a shoulder. "It can't hurt to ask. What kind of forensic scientist are you if you don't check out every lead?"

"I'm too nervous," I admit. "Paul will be here any minute. And I almost got caught that night I broke into the cedar chest as it is."

"Okay, then. I'll do it," Casey says.

My pocket buzzes and I take my phone out to find a text from Paul. He's running late.

"See. It's fate," Casey says. "You want me to do it or what?"

"No. I'll do it. He's *my* dad."

Casey and I spend a few minutes coming up with a better cover story, and I practice what to say. Casey looks up the number and I start dialing.

"Zen," Casey whispers. I take a deep breath and press Call.

"Alumni office," a cheerful voice says. "Once a Bobcat, always a Bobcat. How can I help you?"

"Hi, um, I'm trying to find someone who went to your school," I say. "One of my dad's friends. I want to surprise him. My dad, I mean."

"Okay," the lady on the other end says. "I'll see what I can do to help. Is your dad a member of our alumni association?"

"Uh. I don't think so."

"If you give me his name, I can look it up," the lady says.

Shoot! Casey and I didn't practice for this. I say the only name that comes to mind. "Paul Woods."

"Hmmm, it doesn't appear your dad is a member," the lady says. "I'm not allowed to pass along alumni directory information to you. I'm sorry."

"It's for my dad's birthday and I really want to surprise him. Can you look up his friend's name anyway?"

"I'm sorry. I can't." The lady sounds genuinely sad about it.

"Is there anything you can tell me that might help?"

There's silence on the other end. Did she hang up on me? Casey makes a rolling motion with her hands to tell me to keep going.

"It's really important," I say.

"What's the friend's name?" the lady asks.

I give her my dad's name and the year he graduated. She's typing. It seems like forever before she speaks again.

"We don't have a current address for Michael Wilson," she says. "And even if we did, I couldn't give it to you. But," she says, "I'll give you what we have listed as his hometown. That's the best I can do."

"Oh, yes. Thank you," I tell the lady. She reads me something off her computer and then I hang up.

"What did she say?" Casey says, searching my face.

"My dad's hometown is only forty minutes away."

Casey and I aren't sure *how* this information will be useful. But Casey is positive it will be. "Trust the universe," she says.

Later that night, I find Paul "trusting" something else in the middle of the living room.

"I'm doing a segment where I take a martial arts class," he explains. "I don't want to look like a complete idiot." The second he says this last part, he whacks himself in the head with one of the nunchakus.

"Crap!" he yelps. "It's harder than it looks. I'm supposed to trust the weapon, but all I'm trusting it to do is hit me."

I can't help it, I laugh.

"Don't tell your mom I cursed," Paul says. I tell him I won't.

"Wanna give it a try?" he asks, holding out the weapon. "The video says the trick is to relax your wrist."

I take it and do some figure eights, nice and slow. "Are you supposed to be watching an instructional video ahead of time? I thought the whole point was to go and try new things live on camera."

"Don't tell my boss," Paul says. "I can't get a traumatic brain injury right before I become a father. Or a black eye. I've got to think of my fans."

He's joking. Only probably not about getting a concussion before Boo comes. Mom has been freaking out lately. She keeps having dreams that Paul isn't there for the delivery. Paul says it's more hormone stuff. He and Mom went to a bunch of birthing classes at the hospital, so he probably knows better about it than I do.

I hand the weapon back to Paul. "Here. We learned about glass-breaking patterns in Forensic Science Club today. I'd rather not get caught with these if something gets broken."

Paul frowns and says, "O ye of little faith." I laugh again. Just then, Mom comes in. She gives us some side-eye and says dinner will be ready in ten. Paul takes the nunchakus upstairs and comes back down a few minutes later.

Mom takes one look at his face and says, "What's wrong, honey?"

"I went to put something away in the cedar chest and noticed that the lock is busted," he says sadly. "And there's a gouge in the wood."

"Oh, no! How did that happen?" Mom asks.

Paul shakes his head. "I have no idea."

I hope my voice doesn't give me away. "Can they be fixed?"

"I can probably fill and sand the gouge. But I don't think I can repair the lock. It was a special puzzle that Cole designed. It was meant to fool people into thinking it needed a key." Paul lets out a heavy sigh. "I hate this," he says. "My brother was so proud of the puzzle lock."

Mom wraps an arm around him. "I'm sorry, honey," she says. "Do you think it happened when we moved and we haven't noticed it until now?"

"Possibly," Paul says. "Or it got bumped in the move and suddenly gave way for some reason. I mean, when else could it have happened?"

Paul turns to me. "Felix, have you noticed any damage before now?"

I shake my head. "Nope," I tell him.

Okay. That wasn't a white lie. And it wasn't little.

23

BRAVE

*When we arrive at Forensic Science Club on
Wednesday, Mr. S is wearing a white lab coat
with bloody handprints on it.*

"In honor of Halloween this weekend, we're going to play with
blood," he tells us, and then does an evil laugh.

It's fake blood, of course, but still super fun.

"Make sure you cover your entire work area with newspaper," Mr. S says as we get ready. "And tape it down so it doesn't
move. If the custodian comes after me, I *will* throw you under
the bus, people."

We use medicine droppers to drop blobs of blood onto items
from various heights and angles, and then we measure the results.

Casey is standing on a chair to drop blood from six feet
up. "Be careful," Priya says. "And warn us this time so we can
move out of the way."

The last one, from four feet up and a ninety-degree angle,
made a big spatter. Part of it landed on Priya's shoes.

"Look out below," Casey says.

Ray gets hit in the arm. "Ahhhh. I'm bleeding!" he says in fake panic.

Priya clears her throat. "What's the first rule?" she teases.

Casey, Ray, and I answer at the same time. "Assess, then progress."

"Okay, then," Priya says.

"Excuse me," Ray deadpans. "It appears I am losing blood cells. What should I do next?"

"Well, definitely don't freak out," Casey says. The four of us crack up. And then Priya hands him a tissue.

Awhile later, we experiment with dropping blood onto different surfaces. "The type of surface the blood hits can affect the spatter," Mr. S explains.

The teams each try glass, then tile, wood, and a piece of drywall. The last one is carpet, and we get carried away.

"Yikes," Priya says. "That looks like a murder scene." She laughs. "And my friends think this club sounds boring."

Ray snorts. "That's nothing. My dad says Forensic Science Club is a waste of time."

We stop what we're doing.

"Did he really say that?" I ask.

"Yeah."

"What happened?" Priya asks gently.

"My dad wanted me to do Math Club," Ray begins. "But I lied about when it met, so I could do this instead. Then he found out Math Club doesn't meet on Fridays. He got really mad and said Forensic Science Club was a waste of time and that I should've been doing Math Club all along."

Casey says nothing, just lays her hand on his shoulder. Priya tells him she's sorry. I nod, adding, "Me too."

Ray shrugs. "At least my mom talked him into letting me keep coming. I'm grounded until high school for lying, though."

"That's good. I mean the staying part. Not the grounding part," I say. I think about the things I've learned about my dad since I started doing Forensic Science Club. "And it's not a waste of time." I hold out my fist and Ray gives it a bump.

The four of us go back to dropping fake blood onto the carpet square and measuring spatters. Priya's right. It looks like a murder scene.

With twenty minutes to go, Mr. S announces that it's time to start cleaning up. Everyone gets busy. When the two of us are alone by the sink, Casey and I talk quietly about my dad's hometown.

"Maybe he still lives there," she says.

"I doubt it. How many people live in the same place their whole lives?"

"I have," Casey says. "Besides, it's worth a shot. Have you tried looking him up online yet?"

Even though I don't share Casey's optimism, I tell her I already did.

"His hometown is actually kind of big. There were over two hundred possibilities. Even after I narrowed it down based on age, there were fifty-three Michael Wilsons. It would take me forever to call that many people."

Casey nods. "True. And what would you say, anyway? 'Oh, hello. I'm calling to see if you and your girlfriend had a baby your senior year in college'? That would be awkward."

"Right?" I agree.

"We still have the other things to investigate, though," Casey says. "Getting into the chest was a good idea."

I never told her about damaging the chest with Paul's knife, and I don't tell her about it now, either. Or how Mom followed Paul upstairs to inspect the damage. Or how the two of them were upset and confused.

Or how I lied about it.

"It's almost time to go," Mr. S calls. "You need to hustle if you want time to do a Five-Minute Mystery."

Casey and I agree to talk later. I'm in charge of throwing out the bloody carpet square. The deep red stains remind me of the time I tripped and stumbled headfirst into the edge of a door.

The second I realized blood was oozing from my forehead, I panicked. My mom was usually squeamish when I got hurt, but she got a washcloth, pressed it against my head, and told me everything would be okay. Later, after I'd gotten six stitches and the two of us were heading home from the hospital, Mom told me I was brave.

"You were brave, too," I told her.

She smiled and said, "We can do plenty of hard things when they're for people we love."

I get a lesson in Mom's "we can do hard things for people we love" theory on Saturday. Mom isn't feeling up to it, so I'm taking over her spot to help Paul hand out Halloween candy. Ray and I were supposed to go trick-or-treating together, but he's still grounded.

"Oh, hey!" Paul says as I sit down. "Nice of you to *ketch* up. Get it?"

I give him a frown and look down at the giant ketchup costume Mom bought to go along with Paul's mustard one.

"Ha ha," I say.

Paul and I get our first trick-or-treaters right away, and there's a steady stream of kids for the rest of the night. Everyone seems to enjoy our decorations, especially the cemetery.

Two brothers come up with plastic pumpkin buckets. I can tell they're brothers because the taller one is holding the smaller one's hand to keep him from tripping.

"Trick or treat?" the little dude says.

We give them candy and the older one says, "What do you say?"

"Thank you," the little dude tells us.

Paul and I watch them walk to the end of the driveway.

"Cole used to share his candy with me," Paul says. The name makes my heart sink. Ray got grounded for lying. I'd get grounded, too, if Mom and Paul ever found out what I did. Probably until I'm married.

"Well, I guess *share* might be a strong word." Paul laughs. "He let me have first pick after he sorted his haul into favorites. He hated peanut butter and I loved it, so it worked out well for both of us.

"We were opposites, but boy, he looked out for me." Paul turns to me. "Like you'll look out for Boo."

He's trying to be serious but he's wearing a mustard costume. And despite the guilt, I lose it and bust out laughing.

Paul looks hurt, but then he looks at me and then down at his own outfit. "Yeah. I kind of walked right into that one, didn't I?"

"Yep."

"Well, you gotta *relish* my attempt," Paul says.

I groan and Paul laughs.

A few more trick-or-treaters come by the house. After they leave, Paul turns to me. "Cole loved puns. I wish you could have met him."

"Me too," I say. Guilt is sneaking back in like a cat you've tried to shoo outside.

"He was a good brother." Paul sighs. "I miss him. I guess the damage to the chest really hit me. It's one of the few pieces of him I have left."

I think of my dad's flag football T-shirt, hiding in my closet.

"That makes sense," I say.

"Did I tell you that I found a guy who said he might be able to fix it, or maybe make another custom lock?" Paul asks me.

"That's good, right?"

"It's great," Paul says. "But it won't be the same."

I wonder if I'll ever be the same, either. Or if I'll always feel this ashamed.

24

WRITING INSTRUMENTS

*There are exactly three weeks until Mom and Paul
go to court to change their last names.*

Mom has been addressing envelopes for baby announcements to get a jump on things. I caught her smiling as she wrote *Fine-Woods* all swirly-like in the corners of the envelopes. We're learning about handwriting analysis in Forensic Science Club this week, and Mr. S said emotions can affect handwriting.

For the record, I do not feel swirly-like about it. Mom asked me the other night if I've made a decision about changing my last name, too. How am I supposed to choose? If I don't change my last name, I'll be the odd one out in my own family. But if I do, then my dad might not be able to find me. And he could be my family, too.

"Your handwriting is unique," Mr. S declares on Wednesday. "No one in the world writes exactly like you do. We may learn the same way, but by the time we're teenagers, handwriting is something we don't think about anymore. We develop a style."

Mr. S says "style" with flair and tightens his imaginary tie. We collectively roll our eyes. He writes out the four categories that experts look at when they analyze handwriting.

Letter form: the size and shape of the letters.

Line form: How much pressure was used, and how smoothly do the letters connect?

Formatting: the spacing between letters and words, and things like margins and blank space.

Content: What words did they use? Are there any consistent misspellings or abbreviations?

"All right, everyone," Mr. S says after we've read the categories. "Pop quiz!"

Everyone looks around, confused.

"Relax," Mr. S tells us. "We're going to test our handwriting analysis skills, not our knowledge of biological kingdoms. Take out a piece of paper and a writing instrument. Preferably a pen or pencil. But if you want to use a crayon or an old-timey feathered pen, you do you."

Mr. S has us write the same sentence on two separate pieces of paper:

Forensic Science Club is the bomb diggity.

(None of us know what *bomb diggity* means, but Mr. S says it means "cool" and was popular way before we were born.)

Mr. S gives us each a number to write on the backs of our papers instead of our names. Afterward, he collects them, divides them, and gives the papers from each team to another team to analyze.

The sample I got is interesting. The letters stand straight up, no slant. I notice that the person's capital letters are fancy and not connected to the letters after them, and that their *g*'s have simple curved bottoms. Whoever wrote this also seemed to have pressed fairly hard against the paper.

When we've had some time to examine our samples, Mr. S spreads the second set of samples on the counter in the front. We're supposed to see if we can find the match for the handwriting sample we studied. I find mine right away. A few other people do, too.

"That's not fair," a kid named Joel says. "That person used a pen with purple ink. It's easy to tell which one matches it."

Mr. S claps his hands once and rubs them together. "Ahhh. You've discovered that a person's choice of writing instrument can be a clue," he says. "How many of you have a favorite pen or pencil, or maybe a favorite brand?"

About half of the class raises their hands.

I always grab whatever is closest, so I don't raise my hand. Priya doesn't, either. But Ray and Casey do. I wonder if I know anyone else who has a favorite pen.

Later that night, I ask Mom and Paul if they have favorites.

"Gel pens. Blue ink," Mom says without hesitating. "The only way to go. But if you'd asked me when I was younger, I would've said a four-color retractable pen. Boy, were those a hot commodity."

Paul nudges me. "Well, we know what to get her for Christmas now."

Mom laughs.

"What about you?" I ask Paul.

"Huh. I never thought about it. But I do have a special pen that my parents gave me when I graduated from college," Paul answers. "I use it to sign important things. Like the contract for my first job, and our marriage license. I'm going to use it when we sign the paperwork at the name change hearing, too."

Mom turns to me. "Speaking of that," she says gently. "It's not too late."

"No," I tell her.

"No, you haven't given it more thought, or—"

"I haven't decided."

Mom and I have a staring contest. I can tell she's figuring out how to proceed, but then Paul switches gears on us.

"Hey. I almost forgot," he says. "We have a date for the follow-up interview for my station."

"Oh, yeah?" Mom sounds excited.

"Wait," I say. "What are you talking about?"

"The interview. I told you about it," Mom says.

"No, you didn't," I tell her.

"I'm sure I did."

"No," I say. "I would have remembered something like that."

Mom wrinkles up her brows. "Well, I suppose it's possible I only thought I did. Pregnancy brain is an actual thing, you know."

Paul jumps in. "My station is doing a follow-up story on us. Kind of a 'where are they now.' My boss thought viewers would like to know about Boo."

"Do I have to talk?" I ask.

"No. Just show up and look handsome," Mom says. She turns to Paul. "When is it?"

"Wednesday. I think the station wants to do a live shot for the five o'clock broadcast. The crew will have to set up and we'll need to be ready to go by four-thirty."

"But Wednesday is our second crime scene!" I protest. "I can't leave early."

Paul shakes his head. "Oops. Sorry. Not *this* Wednesday. Next week. But, unfortunately, you'll probably have to miss Forensic Science Club that day, or at least part of it."

"My team needs me. We need all the practice we can get to win and go to the tournament."

"It'll be fine, Felix. I promise," Mom says. "Your team will survive one day without you."

I retreat to my room and complain to Casey.

Well, at least it's not this week, **Casey texts.** And it's fun you'll be on TV.

Been there, done that, **I reply.** Pass.

Oh yeah. The video.

There's a series of three blinking dots from Casey's end.

Hey. You know who might be watching? **she texts.**

Who?

Your dad! You said his hometown is nearby, right? Channel 9 broadcasts all over the state. When we go visit my aunt and uncle in Cleveland, we get it. This might be the perfect chance for him to see you. He'll recognize your mom for sure. She won't be wearing a hat and sunglasses this time, right? lol

She's probably right about my dad recognizing my mom. But she might be wrong about my dad living in his hometown.

It's a long shot, **I text.**

A long shot is still a shot.

I send Casey a rolling-eyes emoji.

She texts back. What's the worst that could happen? Nothing.

There are more dots. Then: What's the best that could happen? Don't text me back until you think about it.

So I do.

My dad could see the news and recognize Mom. He could realize I'm his kid, the son he knew about but never met. And when he sees me, he'll regret not being around. He could call the station and track down Mom.

Okay. You're right, I tell her. Casey sends a dancing bear GIF.

I stretch out in bed. I'm excited about this new possibility, but something keeps poking my brain. It's what Casey said about my dad recognizing my mom. Because it makes me consider something else.

Would my dad recognize *me* if we ran into each other on the street?

25

CRIME SCENE #2

*My team walks down the hill to the high school
building with the rest of the Forensic Science
Club. We file into the band room, which is double
the size of the middle school band room. But the
back half is sectioned off with yellow tape, so
we're kind of cramped together. The high school
forensic science students have set themselves up
in the taped-off space.*

"Attention, everyone," the high schooler in charge says. "A
crime has been committed. The Pioneer was space-napped!"

The Pioneer is the high school mascot. I'm pretty sure
he means the astronaut costume and not an actual person.
Solving the kidnapping of a person would be fun, even it was
staged. Ray told me he heard that the high schoolers get to
solve fake murders where parents and teachers pretend to be
dead.

"Like last time, you'll have twenty-five minutes to walk
around the edge of the scene, sketch and take notes, and talk
to witnesses"—the guy pauses here to cup his hand around

his mouth and stage-whispers, "who may or may n[
perpetrators."

The high schooler reminds us there are two p
unmarked evidence that might help solve the crime
can speak with the Evidence Expert to see if we're rig
Evidence Expert waves some envelopes so we can see
she is.

"Your twenty-five minutes start...now!" the stud
charge says.

We're keeping to the same system we used last tim[
is sketching, I'm taking notes on evidence, Casey is inter\
ing, and Priya is observing everything and helping when
where she's needed. She'll be in charge once we get back t[
classroom.

I find a chair to stand on to get a better view. (Mr. S gi
me some side-eye, but I point to my shirt: LIFE IS SHORT...[
WAIT. THAT'S ME YOU'RE THINKING OF. And he doesn't ma
me get down.) The crime scene looks straightforward. The
are two rows of chairs in the back of the room. Behind tho[
are two bass drums, snare drums, and a gong. A pair of cyn
bals sit in stands on a counter. Next to them is the cap fror
a black marker. It's not labeled. It could just be that some
one has lost the cap to their marker, but I remember the club
motto about nothing being small and decide to ask the Evidence Expert about it. She hands me an envelope. Priya, who's
helping Casey with the interviewing, notices and gives me a
thumbs-up.

I move so I can see into the instrument closet, which is
really more like a small room. There's an open and empty
locker labeled MASCOT. It's marked item A. On the carpet,
in front of the locker, there's a tiny piece of what looks like

wood—part of a toothpick, maybe? Like the marker, it's not labeled as evidence. I ask the Evidence Expert about it and she hands me a second envelope.

Yes!

My excitement is short-lived, though, because Tomás comes up right after me and walks away with an envelope, too.

Once we're back in the classroom, Mr. S hands each team a case file for the Missing Mascot. Before we open it, Casey suggests we should "gather our Zen."

"It worked last time," she says. "We don't want to jinx our system."

"Superstitions aren't real, you know," Ray tells her. Casey stares him down.

"All right. All right," he concedes. "It can't hurt."

We inhale to five and exhale to five on her count. Afterward, Priya lays out the crime scene photos like she's putting together a puzzle and I give a quick summary of the marked evidence.

When I'm done, Priya says, "Okay. Here are the stories Casey and I got from the witnesses." As she recounts each person's statement, Priya holds up their photo.

"Witness number one, Mrs. Wellington, came into the band room about five minutes before second period. She found three students standing inside the instrument closet: witnesses two, three, and four. Witness number two claims to have come early so she could practice and was busy unpacking her bassoon. Witness number three said he was getting his clarinet because he had to leave school for an orthodontist appointment. He was the first person to notice that the astronaut costume was missing. He saw the ransom note attached to the shelf with a

piece of masking tape, removed the note, read it, and handed it to witness number four, who came in next. Then the two of them gave the ransom note to Mrs. Wellington."

"Did either of them say what *they* were doing there early?" Ray asks.

Casey consults her notes. "Witness number three says he's usually early because he has class right down the hall. Witness number four said she came early to see if Mrs. Wellington had time to fix the mouthpiece of her trumpet."

"Hmmm," Ray murmurs.

Beside us, Tomás's team exchanges high fives. It looks like they found their second piece of unmarked evidence.

"Ignore them," Casey says.

Priya motions to the envelopes in my hand. "What did you get, Felix?"

I open them and read out loud. " 'Tests performed on saliva samples from the marker cap indicate DNA from unknown individual.' "

"Well, that's not super helpful," Casey complains. "Read the second one."

" 'Lab tests conclude that the material is *Arundo donax* ("giant cane"), commonly used to make reeds for woodwind instruments. Samples taken from the material match DNA found on the marker pen cap.' "

"They match. That's brilliant!" Casey says. Priya motions for Casey to lower her voice.

"Now we know the same person used both," I say.

"And," Ray says excitedly, "only two of the students play reed instruments."

26

M AND M

"All right," Ray says. "We know it has to be one of these two students." He pulls the photos of witness number two and witness number three forward.

"Are clarinet and bassoon reeds different?" Priya asks Ray. He'd know since he plays clarinet.

"A bassoon uses a double reed," Ray says. "But they're the same material. And we only have a small piece of reed. It's hard to tell."

"Which one is it, then?" Casey asks.

The four of us chew on the question silently. The choice is between two suspects, but we can't just guess. Mr. S makes you explain *how* you solved the crime.

After a while, Priya says, "I think our best bet is to concentrate on the ransom note."

She finds the photo of the ransom note and puts it on the table so we can all read it at the same time. It's written on a piece of wide-ruled notebook paper with a black Magic Marker. The letters are neatly printed.

Greetings, Mrs. Wellington,

I have kidnapped the Pioneer. If you want it back, you will bring sugar cookies (with no sprinkles) for your students on Friday.

Yours truly,

The Mysterious kidnapper (Me)

"That is the nicest ransom note I've ever read," Casey says.

"Do you read a lot of ransom notes?" I tease. She makes a face.

"No, she's right," Priya says. "I mean, it's a friendly-sounding note. I think whoever wrote it did it as a joke. They're asking for cookies."

"And for the whole class," Ray notes.

The case file has writing samples from the students. The notes say they were instructed to print carefully. We examine the ones from our two suspects. Honestly? They both seem similar to the ransom note. A few of the characteristics match one person's sample, while other characteristics seem to match the second person's sample.

"I don't think we can definitely say which person wrote it," Ray concludes.

"What about the words?" I ask. "Remember when we did the thing on handwriting analysis? Content was one of the categories."

Priya grabs her investigative journal and writes down what we tell her:

Greetings / Yours truly
sugar cookies (no sprinkles)
the Mysterious kidnapper (Me)

"The 'no sprinkles' is kind of weird," I say.

Priya speaks up. "Maybe the person doesn't like sprinkles."

"No, wait. I got it," Ray says. "Witness number three said he had an orthodontist appointment."

"And?" Casey says.

"I don't think you're supposed to have sprinkles when you have braces," Ray says. "They'd get stuck. Right?"

None of us have braces, so we don't know for sure. We look around to see if there's someone we can ask and consider how we can do it without giving the solution away. But before we get much further, Tomás's team goes up to the front of the room.

"Attention," Mr. S announces a moment later. "We have our first correct answer."

Ray, Priya, Casey, and I let out a collective sigh.

"Let's see if we're right," Casey says. "We can still come in second."

We send Priya up to present our case. But she comes back shaking her head.

"Shoot," Ray says. "I thought for sure that was right. At least we know it's witness number two."

"But *how* do we know it's her?" Casey asks.

I look over the ransom note again.

Oh, man. How could I have missed that? It's right there!

Casey eyeballs me. "You've got something, don't you?"

"*M* and *M*," I say. "They're both capitalized."

"And?"

"They're the kidnapper's initials. What's witness number two's name?"

"Second place is good," Mom says at dinner.

"And there's one more crime scene, right?" Paul asks. "We're in good shape to go to the tournament." (It's amusing he said "we're," like it's already decided.)

I appreciate that he and Mom are trying to cheer me up. But I'm disappointed that I missed such an obvious clue. The kidnapper wanted to get caught. It was a prank. Witness number two's name was McKenzie Morgan—M.M.

"Yeah, the last crime is in two weeks," I tell Paul. "But I'll miss one of the meetings before that for the TV interview."

"Oh. That reminds me," Mom says. "I bought you a new shirt for that, Felix. It's on your bed. Can you try it on and make sure it fits okay?"

"Sure," I tell her.

"Thanks. I don't want any last-minute wardrobe surprises."

After dinner, I camp out at the kitchen table to work on homework. I can't concentrate. I keep thinking about the crime scene.

I can't believe I didn't see it right away. The initials were *M* and *M*, just like my mom and dad. I open the pictures I took of the stuff in the cedar chest and scroll through to distract myself. When I get to the inscription in the crossword book, something makes me pause.

To M—

Clue: a four-letter word for how I feel about you that starts with L. Don't ya forget!

It was written with a thin blue felt-tip marker. But that's

not what's poking at my brain. Or I don't think that's it. There's something I can't quite put my finger on.

I'm positive I've seen that handwriting and that phrase before. But where?

I decide my brain must be stuck in forensic mode. I'm about to try to get into homework mode, when I suddenly remember *exactly* where I've seen that handwriting before.

27

MIKEY

First, I check to see what Mom and Paul are doing.
They're in their room, packing the hospital bag for
when Boo comes. I don't have a bag because I'm
not going to the hospital. I'm going to Ray's house
instead.

With Mom and Paul busy, I head to the dining room. My heart
pounds as I stand in front of the buffet and dig through the
stacks of loose photos. Only this time, I look at the backs.

About halfway through, I find it.

For M—Love you. Don't ya forget!

It's the same *M*. Tall and tilting to the right. And the same
phrase. *Don't ya forget!*

My dad wrote on the back of this picture. Which must
mean...

I put the rest of the pictures in the buffet. Then I hurry
back to my room and shove my laundry basket in front of the
door.

Adrenaline prickles my skin as I sit down on the bed and pull out the picture.

It's a photo of a young man sitting on a low rock wall. He's smiling and has one arm around a German shepherd. It must be Christmastime because the dog is wearing red-and-green elf ears. The man has brown hair. Like me.

It's my dad.

Michael. Mikey.

I pull up the photo I took of the flag football team picture. It's tiny and hard to see, but I find him there, too. In the back row, off to the left. I zoom in to get a better look.

It's really him.

My dad.

I study the two photos. Besides the same-color hair, my dad and have the same-shaped nose. Our mouths are similar. His eyes look lighter, though. Mine are brown. But we definitely look related.

After all this time, it's weird to be holding a picture of my dad. I study everything I can, like I'm solving a crime.

My dad looks like he was in college when the photo of him sitting on the wall was taken. Maybe a little older. His hair is straight like mine, longish, and parted on the left. Because he's sitting, it's hard to tell how tall he is, but he does look on the short side, like Dr. Ryan told Mom. He's got on a black sweatshirt with Albert Einstein on it. (It's the photo where Einstein is sticking out his tongue.) My dad's also wearing faded blue jeans, and white tennis shoes with gray laces. His right shoelace is undone. Did he know that when the picture was taken?

And the dog. My dad had a dog! I've always wanted one. What was the dog's name? Is it still alive? Probably not. Maybe he has a new one now. Maybe my dad lives in a house with a big backyard for a dog to run around. Where does he live? What does he do for a job? Did he ever get married?

There are so many things I want to know about my dad.

There are so many things I want him to know about me, too.

My earbuds are on my nightstand. I made a playlist with the songs listed on the CD I found in the chest. A lot of them are sappy love songs, and the rest are more pop or rock style. I think you can tell a lot about a person from the music they like. Do they like songs that tell stories? Slow songs? Songs with loud, thumping beats or songs that feel like they're floating down a river?

My dad has good taste. I've liked most of the songs I've listened to so far. And I can tell my dad is one of those people who likes songs with a story. Like the singer is sitting down on their porch, telling you about a time in their life or about something that's happened to them. I can also tell that my dad isn't shy about sharing his feelings, since so many of the songs are about finding and holding on to love.

I stare at the photo I found in the buffet and wonder what happened to my mom and dad. Did they break up just because he wasn't ready to be a dad? If I hadn't come along, maybe they would be together.

The photo doesn't give me any answers. Only an empty feeling.

I put the music on pause and climb off my bed. My dad's flag football shirt is still stuffed in the pocket of my suitcase, in the back of my closest. I've been too nervous to try it on. But now that I know what my dad looks like, I'm feeling braver.

The shirt is too big for me. Not surprising. What is surprising is that the instant I have it on, I feel better. Closer to my dad.

Maybe that's only because I want it to be true.

I go back to my bed, put my earbuds in. And just as I'm about to hit Play, there's a knock at my door.

"Felix?"

Mom!

"It's time for your shot," Mom calls. I can hear her try to turn the doorknob.

I've never moved so quickly in my entire life.

With no time for a better plan, I grab the dress shirt Mom bought me for the interview and throw it on. If Mom catches me wearing the Rabid Squirrels shirt, she'll know I was going through her stuff. And then she and Paul will put two and two together and realize I'm the one who damaged the chest.

My fingers fumble but I manage to get the shirt buttoned. Then I slide the laundry basket away from my door.

"Oh. Hey," Mom says when she sees me. "The shirt fits. Good. Are you ready for your shot?"

"Uh...um..." *Calm down. You're acting weird.* "I need to change first," I tell her.

"Okay," Mom says. "Come downstairs when you're ready."

Whoa. That was close.

But it also gave me an idea.

28

GOING LIVE

*Mom is picking me up right after school on
Wednesday for the interview. I run into Casey on
her way to Forensic Science Club and ask her
to tell the rest of the team I'm sorry, again, for
missing the meeting.*

"Good luck," she says. "Your plan is brilliant. Fingers crossed
it goes well."

I wasn't going to tell anyone, but I ended up needing to
borrow some courage to actually go through with it. Mom and
Paul aren't going to be happy.

The television crew shows up at four-thirty. Although it's
not, technically, much of a crew. It's a reporter, Melanie, and
Paul's usual cameraman, Matt. Mom, Paul, and I sit on the
couch. Mom's in the middle, Paul is on her right, and I'm on
her left.

I tug on the collar of my shirt, which is buttoned to the top
even though Mom said I could undo one or two buttons. She
nudges me and smiles. "Don't look so nervous, Felix. This is
going to be an adventure."

An adventure. Right. And my best chance to find my dad before the court date.

Melanie, Matt, and Paul shoot the breeze a bit since they're friends. Paul mentions the Forensic Science Club.

"There's going to be an inaugural tournament," he says. "Maybe Christy could do a story for the newspaper."

"I'll tell her about it when I get home," Matt says. (Christy is Matt's wife.)

"There'll be a crime scene just for parents to solve, too," Paul adds.

"That sounds fun," Melanie says.

"Doesn't it?" Paul exclaims.

Melanie runs through how the interview will go. Basically, she's going to remind everyone about how Mom and Paul met (the station will replay the videos from the ballpark) and then she'll focus on the impending arrival of Boo. My job is to act like the excited big-brother-to-be. Melanie loves the story behind how Boo got her nickname and she warns me she's going to ask me about it.

Around five-fifteen, Melanie gives us a sixty-second warning from the producer back at the station. Then a ten-second warning. Casey's voice is in my head, counting. I take a deep breath and exhale slowly.

Melanie flashes four fingers, three, two . . . the light on top of Matt's camera goes on.

And we're live.

Melanie and Paul pop on smiles and ease into conversation like it's nothing. Mom smiles, too, but her smile is more nervous. I focus on keeping my face as natural-looking as possible. Casey won't be home in time for the live version, but the story is replaying on the six-thirty news, too.

Paul starts by telling everyone how grateful he feels and how happy we've been since he and Mom got married. He points to Mom's belly.

"And we're excited to share that there will soon be another member of our family," he says.

"Clearly," Mom adds, and the grown-ups laugh like it's the funniest thing.

"How wonderful," Melanie says. "I guess you're giving the diaper-changing thing *a try* instead of your usual segments."

The grown-ups laugh again.

"Do you know if it's a boy or a girl?" Melanie asks, even though she already knows the answer because she and Mom were discussing it before we went on air.

"A girl," Paul says proudly.

"Congratulations," Melanie says. "Do you have a name picked out?"

"Well, we don't have a name settled yet," Mom says. "But for now, her nickname is Boo."

Melanie turns to me. "I hear you're the one responsible for that," she says. "How did you come up with it?"

Everyone is smiling and looking at me. Waiting for a reply. My mouth is suddenly dry as an infield in mid-July. I manage to squeak out a few words. "She was a surprise."

Melanie chuckles. "Well, I think Boo is a perfect nickname, then. It's very clever."

Melanie goes back to speaking with Mom and Paul. I go back to thinking about what I'm going to do. This will hurt Mom and Paul. But what choice do I have?

Melanie is beginning to wrap up.

It's now or never.

I quickly untuck my shirt and begin to unbutton it. Mom

gives me a *What are you doing?* look while she keeps smiling and talking with Melanie.

Right before Melanie starts to thank us and wish us good luck, I wiggle out of the sleeves and slip the dress shirt off.

Mom's eyes grow round when she sees what I'm wearing underneath.

My dad's flag football T-shirt.

29

"OH."

Mom excuses herself the second the light on Matt's camera turns off. Paul is confused, but he thanks Melanie and sees her and Matt to the door. The three of them make a joke about babies having no appreciation for bladders.

When they're gone, Paul glances in my direction but doesn't ask about why I took off my dress shirt. Instead, he knocks on the downstairs bathroom door.

"Honey? Are you okay? Is it the baby?"

Oh, no. I didn't think of that. What if the shock of seeing my dad's shirt makes Mom go into labor or something?

Mom opens the door. "Boo is fine," she tells him. Then she turns to me. "But you're not, mister."

"What's going on?" Paul wants to know.

"What were you thinking, Felix?" Mom asks, her voice tight. "I wouldn't have believed you'd pull something like this. Not in a million years."

The two of us stare at each other. She's angry but I'm angry, too. If she had told me more about my dad when I asked her, none of this would be happening.

"Seriously," Paul says. "Someone tell me what is going on."

Mom's brows knit together. "The shirt."

Paul looks at what I'm wearing again. "Well, it's big on him and ripped, but—"

Mom cuts him off. "It belonged to Felix's father." She's talking to Paul but doesn't take her eyes off me.

"Okay," Paul says. "That doesn't help me here."

Mom takes a step closer to me. "You took something that wasn't yours," she says.

"I didn't take it. I borrowed it," I say. Even I know it's a weak argument.

"You went through my things and took it. What on earth possessed you to think that was acceptable?"

The force of Mom's words surprises me. When she's mad, she usually lowers her voice. Not raises it.

"It...I..."

"Just because you want something doesn't mean you can take it," Mom says, her voice growing louder. "You know better than that."

Paul gently touches her elbow. "Why don't we sit down and talk about this?" he says. "Calmly."

Mom shakes her head. "Don't tell me to be calm. I have a right to be angry."

"Of course you do," Paul says. "That's not what I meant. But getting upset can't be good for you. Or for Boo."

Mom glares at me. I can't remember the last time I saw her this upset. Maybe when I was four and wandered off at a playground. Mom couldn't find me for fifteen minutes and by the time she did, her face was red and I swear I could see a vein on her forehead beating. But that was more fear than anything else. This isn't fear.

"Tell him," Mom says to me.

I jut out my chin.

"Tell him, Felix," Mom says. "Tell Paul where the shirt was. You owe him the truth."

She already knows where the shirt was. I don't know why she's making me say it out loud.

"I'm so confused," Paul mutters.

I wait. But Mom does, too.

Half a minute—maybe a full minute—passes. Something inside me loosens. I hadn't thought about what it was going to feel like when Paul found out the truth. I guess part of me was hoping he never would.

I lower my head and look at Paul's shoes. "I got the shirt out of the chest. In your bedroom."

There's silence as a few seconds tick by. And then Paul understands.

"Oh."

That's all. One little syllable and I know he knows I was the one who damaged Cole's beautiful cedar chest. One of the things he cherishes the most. Even though I'm not looking at him, I know Paul is looking at me. His pain is like a piece of invisible string between us.

"I'm sorry," I tell him.

Paul doesn't say anything. It's worse than Mom yelling.

It's Mom who breaks the silence. "You need to go to your room," she says. "I don't feel like being around you at the moment."

Mom has said this before to me. It's her way of letting me know that I've crossed a line and should get out of her sight for a while if I know what's good for me. (Not that she's ever spanked me or anything.)

I don't feel like being around her at the moment, either. She hasn't asked a single thing about *why* I did what I did. Isn't she even the tiniest bit curious why I wore my dad's T-shirt on live television?

I go to my room and wait. Wait to be punished. Wait for Mom to yell at me some more. Wait for Paul to tell me how disappointed he is. Wait to feel better.

When none of those things happens, I text Casey and fill her in on everything, including what I did to the cedar chest.

I feel terrible. Mom and Paul hate me.

They don't hate you. They're upset right now. They'll get over it. It's like a law for parents.

She adds a smiley face but it doesn't help.

I shouldn't have worn the shirt.

But you had to. You already said your mom wouldn't tell you anything about your dad.

I broke Cole's lock and scratched the wood.

But you didn't mean to.

I consider this long enough that Casey texts a question mark, wondering if I'm still here.

That's true, I finally text back.

There's another long pause.

She didn't even ask me why I did it, I text eventually.

Casey responds with a sad-face emoji.

I send multiple texts in a row.

It didn't matter to her that I had a reason.

She doesn't care that I want to meet my dad.

All she cares about is a piece of furniture.

And that I lied and took something.

All she cares about is the new baby and Paul.

That last one isn't true, **Casey responds.**

Fiiiiine, **I type.**

But the rest of them are, **I add.**

Casey says she has to go and that we can talk more tomorrow. I take off my dad's shirt, fold it, and put it back in the suitcase in my closet. I don't know if Mom will demand I give it back now that she knows I have it. I hope she doesn't.

And I hope Paul knows that wanting to meet my dad has nothing to do with him. I let him down. And for what? Ten seconds of airtime wearing a shirt on television.

For a dad who probably wasn't even watching.

30

TIME

I skipped dinner. Mom brought me a plate of food and left it outside my door like I'd ordered room service at a hotel. She left a note to remind me to bring the dishes downstairs and put them in the dishwasher.

We've managed to avoid each other since. But we're stuck with each other now as we head toward Mom's baby check appointment. She didn't say why she wanted me to come along. I'm guessing she wants to trap me in the car and yell at me some more.

At least she brought me a snack. I have a handful of trail mix in my mouth when she starts talking.

"How was school? Oh. Sorry. Finish chewing first," she says, looking in the rearview mirror at me in the backseat.

"It was okay," I tell her.

"Got lots of homework?"

"Some," I say. "Not much."

"Maybe you can do it while I'm with the doctor."

"It's hard to work without a table."

"There are end tables," Mom says. "You could use one of those."

"Sure."

I'm not in the mood for pretending everything is fine. Yesterday, Casey tried to cheer me up. (Ray could see that something was up but gave me space.) I'm upset Mom hasn't asked for my side of the story yet. Does she hate my dad so much that she *never* wants to talk about him?

Mom must not be in the mood to pretend, either, because she turns on the radio and doesn't say anything the rest of the way to the doctor's office.

The waiting room is full of pregnant ladies. There are a few men, too, but no other kids. Unless you count a baby in a stroller. I peek at it when we walk by. He (or she, I can't tell) is surrounded by blankets. Like he's an egg that the mom is afraid is going to roll away.

I start my homework on my lap, not on an end table like Mom suggested. I make it through six problems. "What's taking so long?" I ask.

Mom stretches her legs. "Maybe the doctor had a delivery. Babies don't generally come when it's convenient. It's kind of their thing."

"Isn't there more than one doctor?"

"Yes, but moms like to have someone they know deliver their babies."

"Why are we even here?" I ask.

"I'm getting checked."

One time, Mom told me her doctor uses a tape measure to measure her belly like Dr. Ryan measures me. I wonder how much it will have grown this time. Because, even though I'd never say it to her face, Mom looks huge.

Finally. The nurse calls Mom's name. Mom holds out her

hands and I get up to give her a pull. After she's gone, I sit back down to finish up my homework.

The baby in the stroller cries. His mom picks him up. He's so tiny!

Will Boo be that small and fragile?

The mother holds the baby with one arm and lays out a blanket on the empty part of the padded bench she's on with the other hand. Next, she gently lays the baby down and then *fold over, fold up, wrap*—the baby looks like a burrito. He stops fussing.

"It's a parenting trick," the mother says to me when she notices I'm watching. "Would you like to learn?"

I nod and walk over. She unwraps the baby and then wraps him up again, going slower this time and explaining what to do. I thank her and she smiles back.

Mom comes waddling into the waiting room half an hour later.

"Ready?" she asks. I don't answer, just get up and follow her out.

Pretty soon, we're back in the car, heading home. Mom eases onto the highway, and the second we're in the right lane coasting along, she lowers the volume on the radio.

"Can we talk about what happened Wednesday?" she asks.

"Guess so," I tell her. At least I'll be able to explain why I wore the shirt. And ask her if she knows how to get in contact with my dad. And, more importantly, will she?

Mom clears her throat. "You understand that what you did was wrong, don't you?"

"I'm sorry I took the shirt without asking."

Mom nods. "Thank you for the apology."

"What's my punishment?"

"There is no punishment," Mom says.

I'm confused. Mom hasn't grounded me in a while, but I figured I'd have to at least clean the bathrooms or do extra chores or something. Being punished would be better than feeling guilty.

Mom goes on. "You're eleven. Old enough to learn that sometimes sorry isn't enough. You broke my trust and, just as importantly, you broke Paul's trust. You could've told him the truth when it happened, or when we noticed the damage."

"I didn't want to get in trouble."

"Owning up to things is hard," Mom says. "But it's the right thing. You make a mistake, you fix it."

She's one to talk about owning up to things. She *still* hasn't asked me why I took the T-shirt.

"Do you even want to know why I did it?" I ask. It comes out more meanly than I meant it to.

Mom glances at me in the rearview mirror.

"It doesn't matter," she says.

"It matters to *me*!"

She grips the steering wheel tighter. "No. What matters now is that you make things up to Paul. You hurt his feelings. And you broke our trust. That's going to take some time to rebuild."

Great. Time is something that's already in short supply.

There are only ten days until Mom and Paul's court date.

I still don't know if I'm going to change my name. All I know is that I want to give my dad the chance to get to know me. Before I have to decide if I'm going to become somebody else.

31

GIVING IT A TRY

The crib Mom and Paul special-ordered for Boo came last week. The box has been sitting in the dining room, much to Mom's frustration. On Sunday, she comes to my room and asks if I'll help Paul with it.

It's less of a question and more of a request, though. "Paul needs a hand with the crib," she says. "If you're not busy."

I find Paul in the dining room, dragging the crib box across the floor.

"Need an extra hand?" I ask.

He pauses before he answers. "Sure. That'd be great."

Paul positions himself at the back of the box so he can push, while I set myself at the front to help pull it. When we get it to the bottom of the stairs, we stop to figure out how to proceed. The box is too wide to lay down on the stairs. We end up dragging it vertically, like we've been doing. Paul pushes from the bottom and I pull and direct the box from the top. There's a slight turn when we get to the landing, but we manage.

"You're getting stronger," Paul says. "The shots must be working."

"Guess so," I tell him.

At my appointment last month, I hadn't grown much. I didn't care. But Dr. Ryan upped my dose.

Paul and I lay the crib box on the carpet in the nursery and unpack the pieces. I help him check to see if everything is there.

"Okay," he says, reading the directions. "Step one. Panic."

"It doesn't say that," I say.

Paul smiles. It's a small one. "Nah. You're right. But it might as well," he says, gesturing at the piles of screws, nuts and bolts, and pieces of wood. "Let's give it a go, though."

"Hey. You're a poet and didn't know it," I say, because that's what we say in our family when someone accidentally makes a rhyme. This gets another small smile.

Paul's trying to give me a chance to try and fix things between the two of us. Which I appreciate. Things have felt weird ever since the night of the interview. He's done a good job avoiding me, and when we see each other he hasn't said more than a few sentences.

Today isn't any different. The two of us work with few words. And they're mostly about needing a certain screw or tool or assembly piece.

No jokes.

No asking me what's going on at Forensic Science Club or talking about the tournament.

No mention of the interview or me secretly wearing my dad's flag football shirt.

"What's your next Give It a Try Guy segment on?" I ask.

Paul frowns at the half-finished crib in front of us. "Uh. I'm tagging along in a salt truck next week if it snows like it's supposed to."

"That sounds interesting," I tell him.

"It was from a viewer," he says, distracted. "People like to pass along ideas."

Before I can ask him more about it, Paul tosses the instruction booklet on the floor.

"Cole was the one who could put anything together," he says.

My heart sinks into my stomach. I think about breaking into the chest. And Paul's "Oh" when he put two and two together.

I open my mouth to say "I'm sorry." Again. For the hundredth time, it seems. But Paul looks at me.

"You know what? I can figure the rest of this out myself," he says.

"Are you sure?"

"Yes."

"Because I can stay," I tell him. "I don't mind."

"No, really," Paul says. "I've got this. You can go."

That's when I realize he's not telling me I can leave. He's asking me to.

On Monday, we learn about jimmy marks in Forensic Science Club.

"These are the marks left behind by tools during a crime. Technically, they're called impressions," Mr. S says. "Speaking of impressions, does anyone want to hear mine of the economics teacher from the movie *Ferris Bueller's Day Off*?"

No one knows what he's talking about.

"Anyone? Anyone?" he says. "All right. Your loss. It's a good one."

Instead of an impression, we get a mini-lecture on impressions and how they're often useful in crime solving.

"Tools leave marks when they're used against something soft, like wood," Mr. S says. "They can leave scratches when they rub or slide against a surface. Or leave distinctive slice marks when they're used to cut wires or other items."

I never thought of wood as soft before. It feels solid and strong, and it sure hurts when you stub your toe against a table. But solid and strong things can still be damaged.

Mr. S hands each team a piece of wood and five tools: a flathead screwdriver, a Phillips head screwdriver, a small crowbar, a hammer, and a butter knife. We're supposed to match the impressions, or jimmy marks, with the tool that made them.

"All right," Priya says. "Let's do this by process of elimination."

Casey, Priya, and I watch as Ray picks up the tools one at a time and tries to match the tool to the damage in the board. It's not as easy it sounds. But we figure out that the crowbar made the biggest cut. The hammer one wasn't too hard, either, because it left clear, round indentations. ("The face. That's what the part that hits things is called," Ray explains. "In art camp, we made sculptures using recycled tools.")

We're trying to figure out which jimmy mark was made with the Phillips head screwdriver. I can't help but think about the mark I left in the lid of Cole's chest.

"Earth to Felix," Casey says, waving her hand in my face.

"Sorry."

"Don't space out on us," she says.

"Yeah," Ray adds. "We need to work as a team. Especially on Wednesday. Points-wise, we're neck and neck with Tomás's team."

Like anyone has to remind me. Assuming both teams find the unmarked evidence on Wednesday and get the maximum points for teamwork, whoever solves the case first will go to the tournament.

We have to go.

Casey wants to win her own trophy. And even though neither of them has said anything out loud, I know Ray wants to prove to his dad that Forensic Science Club isn't a waste of time, and Priya wants to show her friends that science can be cool.

And I want to give Paul the chance to solve the crime scene for parents.

Because if I do, maybe it'll help make up for what I did.

32

CRIME SCENE #3

On Wednesday, Mr. S tells everyone to grab their
coats and head outside. Our last crime scene is
set up at the high school. It's windy and a few
snowflakes are falling as we head down the hill.
We're supposed to get several inches of snow by
tomorrow morning. I know this because Mom
was complaining about having to drive to
Dr. Ryan's office later. My appointment is at 6:15.
The office is open late on Wednesdays. (Lucky me.)

The representatives from the high school forensic science class are already at the scene.

"Welcome to your final crime scene," one of them announces, waving his arm at the blocked-off area behind the school building.

"Today, it's the Case of the Jealous Artist," he says. He goes on to tell us what happened, and finishes by explaining, "You'll have twenty-five minutes to observe and sketch the crime scene. Your witnesses and potential suspects are over there." A group of seven high schoolers stands off to the side. They wave. "As usual, there are two pieces of evidence that aren't marked but may or may not help solve the crime. So, keep your eyes open. Good luck. And . . . go!"

This is it. Time to get into the tournament.

Because there are seven witnesses-slash-potential-suspects, Casey and Priya are teamed up to do the interviews. Ray walks along the perimeter, stopping every ten feet to sketch. I'm walking the perimeter in the opposite direction and taking notes on the marked evidence.

We were told that the crime took place after the art students spent class time outside, doing their own versions of Jackson Pollock paintings in a grassy area. (Pollock was the artist who splashed and dripped paint on his canvases. "It's called action painting," Ray told us.) There are five large canvases spread out on the ground, covered in spatters of bright paint. One painting only has shades of blue, though, except for a giant blob of yellow paint in the middle and a smaller blob off to one edge. It must be the vandalized painting because it's tagged as item A.

"See if you can make a decent guess about the diameter of the yellow splat," Ray whispers when the two of us pass each other. "It might be useful."

"Got it," I whisper back.

By the time I make my way over to the art cart and ladder, it's almost time to go. I take notes on the different cans of acrylic paint and brushes. I notice spatters of dried paint on the wooden ladder leaning against the wall by the back door. Red, yellow, purple, blue, green. It looks like our step stool after Paul dripped when we painted the nursery. Only that was one color, Wishful Green. Back when Paul wasn't disappointed in me.

After twenty-five minutes, we head back up the hill to the middle school. The teams talk quietly as we walk. Ray, Priya, Casey, and I "gather our Zen" along the way so we can get started the second we get to the room. There's a lot riding on the outcome of this crime scene. For all of us.

The case file has more pictures than the last two cases did. Casey helps Priya spread them out. We use Ray's sketch to position them so they're as close to the actual crime scene as possible.

Then we assess what we already know.

"What did the witnesses say?" I ask.

Priya checks her notes. Casey follows along with her own in case she got something Priya didn't.

"The art teacher reported that she and five students went outside during third period," Priya says. "The students were working on their individual projects for the Winter Art Fair. The teacher walked around, commenting on each piece. At the end of third period, everyone went inside, washed their hands in the art room, and went to lunch. When they came back out, one of the canvases"—Priya holds up the photo of item A—"had spatters of yellow paint."

"Why did they come back instead of going to their next period?" Ray asks.

"They all had permission to miss their next class and keep working," Casey reports.

"Which means whoever did this knew they had to do it during lunch," Ray says.

"Or right before," I say. "Did everyone go to the art room to wash up at the same time?"

Casey consults her notes. "The art teacher said everyone walked together but that artist number one forgot his coat, which he took off to keep clean, and had to go back. And his painting wasn't ruined at that point."

"He was the artist? I guess we can move his picture into the 'Not It' pile, then," I say. Priya sets the photo aside.

Priya reads from her notes. "The students all claim to have been in the cafeteria when the damage presumably occurred. The art teacher said she was in her classroom doing an interview with a student writing a story on the art show for the school newspaper."

The crime scene might be fake, but the Winter Art Fair isn't. (Ray is working on a piece for it.) There would definitely be a story about it in the school newspaper.

Wait. The newspaper!

Not the school newspaper. The big one, the *Columbus Dispatch*.

Casey said Channel 9 could be seen at her aunt and uncle's house, which is two hours away. It's broadcast across the state. The *Dispatch* is probably delivered all over the state, too.

I bet if my team got into the tournament, Matt's wife, Christy, would do a story like Paul suggested. And a newspaper story would be way better than a few minutes on TV because it would last longer. If my dad still lives *anywhere* in Ohio, there'd be a better chance he'd see it. And maybe the newspaper would put in our picture. My dad might not recognize me, but he'd recognize my last name. He'd wonder if I was related to Marcy Fine, and then put it together. And since the article would say where I go to school, he could reach out to me. Or Mom. He'd probably go to her first.

Hold on. What if Dad reaches out to Mom and Mom doesn't tell me? She wouldn't do that, would she?

I don't have time to stop and think about it.

Off to our left, I can hear Tomás's team getting excited about something.

Okay. Let's do this. We've *got* to solve this crime first.

33

TRUST THE UNIVERSE

"Hold on," I say. "Were there any other witnesses?"

"The custodian," Priya says.

"What did he say?"

Casey takes over for the moment. "He reported that he'd left the ladder out because he planned to use it in the afternoon. He noticed it had been moved. In fact, he made a big fuss about it. He said, 'Why can't people leave their hands off other people's things?'"

Ray jumps in. "It was moved? Do you suppose it could be one of the unmarked pieces of evidence?"

Casey frowns. "How can something being moved be evidence? We can't *see* that something was one place and then another unless we saw it being moved."

"Well, maybe we can," Ray says. He closes his eyes.

"What are you doing?" Casey asks, clearly annoyed.

"Can't talk. Visualizing."

Casey sighs. Priya and I wait.

A few seconds later, Ray's eyes pop open. "Prints," he whispers excitedly.

Priya grabs the right photo and says, "But there aren't any shoe prints nearby."

"No, not shoe prints—"

I see where he's going and interrupt. "Indentations in the grass from the legs of the ladder," I whisper excitedly.

The four of us check the photos. It's hard to see any indentations, but there's mud on one of the ladder legs.

Ray and I walk up to the front of the room where the high schooler who's acting as the Evidence Expert sits. We tell him our theory about the ladder being an unmarked piece of evidence, and he hands us an envelope.

"Yes!" Casey and Priya quietly cheer as we walk back to the table.

Since it was Ray's catch, we let him open the envelope. Inside are a lab report and a closeup photo of the ladder. It's clear from the marks in the grass that it's been moved. There's a tiny spatter of green paint on the bottom step.

Ray reads the lab results. As he does, his face falls. "Aww. No useful fingerprints were on the ladder. No useful shoe prints on or near it, either. It's a dead end."

"Hold up," Priya says. "Maybe not. Look, that green paint is wet. It's shiny."

She motions for us to lean in closer. "Remember what we learned when we spattered blood? The higher the height, the bigger the spatter."

Ray grabs the photo of the damaged painting and lays it down for everyone to see.

"Look," Priya continues. "The yellow spatter spreads out like it was dropped from high up—"

Now it's Ray's turn to interrupt. "Felix, what was your estimate for the splat in the middle of the painting?'

I tell him.

"Are the paint spatters on the other canvases that big?" Casey asks.

The four of us check and discover they aren't.

"Whoever dumped the yellow paint must have done it while standing on the ladder," Priya concludes.

Ray frowns. "Okay. So, we know the perpetrator used the ladder. Without prints, that's not super useful."

"He's right," Casey says. "How is that helpful?"

"I don't know," Priya says. "But maybe we're missing something. We should see if there's anything that ties one of the witnesses-slash-suspects to the ladder."

Each of us grabs one of the photos of the witnesses to examine more closely. I end up with the picture of the artist whose painting was ruined. It obviously wasn't him, but maybe I'll find something useful.

There's nothing out of the ordinary in his photo. The artist is wearing jeans, a long-sleeved T-shirt, and a smock, just like the other artists. The smock is speckled with various shades of blue (like the ones in his painting) and some red and yellow. The artist's shoes are speckled with paint, too.

A few minutes later, everyone lays their photos down.

"Find anything?" Ray asks hopefully.

Casey, Priya, and I shake our heads.

We're quiet for a moment. Then Ray asks, "What about motive?"

"Motive is for detectives, not forensic scientists," Casey reminds him.

He scowls. "I *know*," he says. "But what if there's something we missed in the witnesses? Let's go over them again."

"Fine," Priya says.

She tells us that the four artists are top students, hoping to win the grand prize ribbon at the Winter Art Fair. The teacher had positive things to say about all the paintings, but everyone agreed it sounded like artist number three got the best feedback.

"But it was artist number one whose painting was ruined," Casey says. "That doesn't make sense if we're looking at motive."

Tomás is going up to talk with the Evidence Expert. Shoot! If his team gets the solution first, they'll be in the tournament. I won't get my picture in the newspaper. And that'll be that. Mom and Paul will go to court next week and change their last names and I won't ever find my dad.

I've got to do something.

"Trust the universe." That's what Casey said when I found out my dad's hometown and didn't know how it would be useful. I'd had the idea to wear the Rabid Squirrels T-shirt on live TV, which didn't work.

But maybe it was because the universe had something else in mind.

34

TWO VOICES, ONE BAD IDEA

Tomás and his team are huddled at their table.
They read what was in the envelope from the
Evidence Expert and set it aside. They know the
second piece of unmarked evidence. But what
they don't know is what I've noticed.

The piece of paper with the unmarked evidence was knocked off the table and fell to the floor.

Any minute, Tomás and his team are going to walk up to Mr. S and present their findings. I have to act *right now*.

My body works faster than my brain, and I stand up.

"Where you going?" Priya asks, as surprised as I am.

I wave my pencil. "Sharpener."

"Well, do it quickly. We need you."

Adrenaline pumps through my body as I make my way toward the other side of the room. When I pass Tomás's table, I don't even look at the piece of paper on the ground. Instead, I step on it and carefully slide it along the floor under my left shoe. This way, if I get caught, I can say I didn't know it was there. Like I accidentally stepped on it and it got stuck, like toilet paper.

I stand at the sharpener, whittling my pencil down while I decide what to do. Two voices battle back and forth in my head.

Voice one: *It would be wrong to look at the piece of paper. We didn't find the second piece of evidence, the other team did.*

Voice two: *But your team is going to find the second piece of unmarked evidence any second anyway. This is just taking a shortcut.*

Voice one: *It's cheating. I don't want to win this way.*

Voice two: *You want to go to the tournament, right? Come on. The end justifies the means.*

Voice one: *I can't do it.*

Voice two: *This could be your last chance to meet your dad. And you broke Cole's chest, so you've already broken the rules. Do it.*

Voice one: *I'll get caught.*

Voice two: *Not if you stop thinking about it and look at the piece of paper already!*

My hands are shaking and I drop my pencil for real. I check the room to see if anyone is paying attention, and then I squat down and turn the paper over.

It's a close-up photo of one of the artist's shoes. There's a green thumb-size smudge on the toe of one of them. I recognize those shoes. They're the ones I saw a few minutes ago when I looked at the picture of the artist whose painting was destroyed. But that would mean . . .

"Hey!" a voice says.

I look up and find Tomás standing there.

"That's our evidence. You're cheating. Mr. S!"

Mr. S doesn't mince words. "I'm sorry. Your team is disqualified. Please take your seats and wait for the other teams to finish solving the case."

Priya looks like someone pushed her down a flight of stairs. "Disqualified," she says when the four of us are at our table. "I can't believe it."

"Why, dude?" Ray asks me. "We could've won on our own. We were getting close."

"And now we don't get to go to the tournament," Priya says. She sounds as disappointed as Mr. S did when he called me and Tomás to the front and I admitted what I'd done.

"I'm sorry," I tell them.

"A whole lot of good that does us," Ray says.

"I messed up, okay?"

"It's not okay," Priya says. "*Your* mistake cost the rest of us the chance to go to the tournament."

Ray shakes his head. "I don't get it."

"It was an accident," I say.

"How can looking at piece of paper under your shoe be an accident?" Ray wants to know.

"It was just there. I didn't know what it was until I looked at it." I'm surprised how easily the lie comes flying out. But even I realize how fake it sounds.

Casey hasn't said anything this whole time. I look at her. "I had a reason," I tell her.

She shakes her head and then lays it down on top of her hands on the table, her face turned away from us. It feels as bad as Paul's "Oh" when he found out I was the one who damaged the chest.

"I really wanted to go to the tournament," I tell my team.

"We all did," Ray says.

After that, there's nothing else to say. We wait to see what happens while Priya gathers up the notes and photos and puts them neatly back into the case file folder.

In the end, Tomás and his team solve the crime first, which means they'll be going to the tournament. They figured out that the green smudge of paint on the artist's shoe was from yellow and blue paint mixed together. Artist number one had destroyed his own painting in order to blame the other artists and get his competition kicked out of the art show.

When time is up, Casey is the last one to leave the class-room. I wait for her out in the hall.

"I'm sorry," I say when she comes walking out. She keeps marching.

"I'm sorry," I repeat. "Please listen."

She stops but doesn't turn around.

I know she's upset about missing her shot at her own tro-phy and outshining her older sister for once. But she's got to understand. She's the only person I've told about looking for my dad. The only one helping me. I know she'll get it, so I try to explain. "I thought if we got to go to the tournament, the newspaper would do a story. And maybe my dad would see it."

She turns to face me now. When she speaks, her voice is cool and composed. "Well, you blew it for both of us, then, didn't you?"

She starts to walk away again, and I try to follow her.

"Leave me alone, Felix. We're not friends anymore."

35

UNRAVELING

*When I get in the car, Mom doesn't ask about
how the final crime scene went. She takes one
look at my face, and I guess she doesn't have to.*

It's snowing harder than it was earlier. Mom flips on the windshield wipers. The two of us listen to the *whish-whoosh, whish-whoosh.*

In my head, I hear Casey's words over and over in the rhythm of the wipers. *"Not friends. Not friends. Not friends."* My heart is a ball of yarn and someone has tugged the end loose.

When we arrive, there's only one other person in Dr. Ryan's waiting room. The receptionist asks Mom how the roads are, and Mom says they're not too bad yet.

"Kind of quiet around here," Mom observes.

"We've gotten multiple cancellations," the receptionist says. "They're saying five inches of snow. And ice to boot!"

Mom frowns. "Really? That's not what they said on the

news this morning. I guess I should have listened to an update."

Mom and the receptionist joke about how if other people were as accurate as meteorologists, they'd lose their jobs.

Nurse Susan comes to get us before we're even done signing in.

"How are you doing?" she asks Mom.

"Good. *Ooomph*." Mom rubs the side of her belly.

"Baby kicking?" the nurse asks.

"More like doing taekwondo," Mom says. I wonder how there's even space in there for Boo to move, let alone kick.

"What about you, Felix?" Nurse Susan asks. "School going well?"

"It's good," I answer politely. *Except that I cheated and blew my whole team's shot at going to the forensic science tournament right before we came here,* I add in my head.

When we get to the room where kids are measured, Nurse Susan has me slip off my shoes and stand against the wall to record my height. Afterward, she has me stand on the scale. As usual, she doesn't give us the numbers, since Dr. Ryan likes to be the one to tell you. She shows us to an exam room.

Mom takes the chair. I sit on the examination table and look out the window. Outside is gray. Everything on the inside is gray, too.

I shouldn't have cheated. I didn't even have to. I saw that green paint smudge on the artist's shoe. I could've put it together if I'd tried. Or waited a few minutes.

Now I've blown everything for everyone. Especially me and Casey.

There's a quick knock on the door before Dr. Ryan comes

strolling in. After he finishes washing his hands, he sticks one out toward me. I shake it.

"It's good to see you again, Felix," he says. "How are things going?"

"Fine," I lie.

"Splendid. Let's see where we are." Dr. Ryan uses his thin red measuring tape to collect measurements of my head, arms, and legs. He listens to my heart and peeks in my throat, and down my pants and under my arms to see if I'm growing any hair yet. (I could've told him I'm not.)

"Well, do you want the good news or the good news?" he asks.

Mom laughs. "We'll take the good news," she says.

Dr. Ryan turns to me. "It looks like we can stay with the current dosage for now. As for the second piece of good news, Felix, you've put on six pounds and grown a whole inch in the last three months."

"Oh, that's wonderful!" Mom says.

"What do you think, Felix?" Dr. Ryan says. "At this rate, you're looking at at least four inches in the next year."

Dr. Ryan looks like he just told me he was giving me a million dollars.

Four inches? But then I won't be short anymore. I like being short. It makes me different. I have a collection of funny T-shirts and comebacks and an awesome nickname. My dad is short.

The ball of yarn inside my chest drops to the floor. And then whoever's in charge of these things suddenly kicks it across the room. I can feel it unraveling. Everything flashes before my eyes.

Noticing that Tomás dropped the clue.

Walking over to the pencil sharpener.

Debating. Looking.

Seeing Mr. S's disappointed face when I admitted I cheated. Getting my team disqualified.

Standing in the hall after Casey said, "We're not friends anymore."

Blowing Paul's chance to solve the crime scene for parents.

Losing my last chance to find my dad.

It's. All. Too. Much. And now Mom and Dr. Ryan are watching, waiting for me to say something, to be happy about growing an inch.

I swallow hard. And burst into tears.

36

THINGS THAT GO *THUMP*

*Dr. Ryan grabs a box of tissues while Mom hugs
me and apologizes for my reaction.*

My doctor shakes his head. "Don't worry about it," he says mildly. "I've seen it all."

Dr. Ryan pats my shoulder and when I look up, he says, "At least you didn't throw up on me. One time, I was even bitten. If you can believe that."

Mom laughs, and I wipe my snot on the tissue she's handed me.

"Again. I'm so sorry," Mom says. "Usually it's me who's crying at the drop of a hat."

Dr. Ryan waves her off. And then he looks me right in the eye.

"You're doing fine. This is new," he says. "And new things can sometimes feel overwhelming."

After I collect myself and assure everyone I'm okay, Dr.

Ryan says he'll see us in a month. Nurse Susan brings our paperwork.

"Next time you come in," she says, "you'll probably be lugging a car seat with a newborn."

"I sure hope so," Mom says.

Outside, the snow is coming down hard. The parking lot is already covered in white, and I let Mom hold on to my shoulder as we walk to the car. I guess it's the perfect night for Paul to do his ride-along as a salt truck driver. And at least I won't have to tell him about what happened at Forensic Science Club right away. Even though he's mad at me, he wished me luck this morning.

I'm tired from crying. And it's cold. I offer to press Mom's seat warmer button for her since Boo's in the way, but she waves it off. "My back is bothering me," she says. "The cold seat might help."

It takes way longer than usual to get home. We pass three fender benders. "For Pete's sake," Mom complains. "It's snow, people! It's what happens when water freezes." I guess her back must hurt because she isn't usually this cranky.

Mom warms up chicken noodle soup for dinner. Since she can't get comfortable on the hard kitchen chairs, we set up TV trays in the living room and eat on the couch.

We turn on a game show. There's a running list of school closures along the bottom of the screen. It's smaller districts, though. Not mine.

"You think you guys will get a snow day tomorrow?" Mom asks. "That would be exciting."

When I don't immediately answer, she pretends to be me. "'Why yes, Mother, a snow day would be exciting.'"

I look at her.

"Come on. That was funny," she says.

"I thought bad jokes were Paul's department."

"Well, he's not here," she says, patting my knee. "Someone's gotta do it."

She motions for me to grab an extra pillow and I help her get comfortable.

A few minutes pass and she asks, "So, do you want to talk about happened at Forensic Science Club?" I panic, thinking that Mr. S called and told her what I did. But she doesn't look angry. Only curious.

"Not really," I say.

"How about what happened at Dr. Ryan's? Want to talk about that?"

"Definitely not."

"Okay," Mom says. "I'm here if you change your mind."

It's nice she's trying to cheer me up. Especially since I know she's still upset with me about breaking her and Paul's trust. But I can't fix any of it. Especially not cheating and blowing my last shot to find my dad.

I know eventually I'll have to come clean. But right now, I need things between my mom and me to be okay.

Mom and I watch TV for a while. Her phone buzzes around eight o'clock. "Paul says he's going to be out all night doing the road warrior segment," she lets me know.

That's okay with me.

Tonight, it can be just the two of us.

I'm having a bad dream. Mom is somewhere in a creepy house calling my name over and over. I hear moaning, but I can't tell where (or who) it's coming from. Nurse Susan is there, too, and she's carrying a giant needle and saying, "You've grown a whole inch!"

Something thumps.

Only it's not in my dream. I'm awake, my ears straining.

Thump.

Someone's downstairs. In the kitchen. Paul? I crawl out of bed and peek out the window. A blanket of snow covers the driveway and there aren't any tire marks. My alarm clock says it's 1:18 a.m.

I inch toward my door, open it, and listen harder. There's a shuffle. Someone is moving stuff around on a shelf.

Mom's bedroom door is closed. She must be asleep. There are more shuffling noises, and a door opening. Would a burglar steal stuff from the pantry?

I go full ninja down the stairs. Minus the sword, of course. Or a weapon of any kind, for that matter. What am I going to do if it really is an intruder? I did *not* think this through.

I reach my arm around the kitchen doorway and flip the light switch anyway.

"Oh! Felix! You scared the bejesus out of me," Mom says, her hand flying to her chest. She's standing in front of the open fridge, wearing an extra-long flannel shirt, a bathrobe, and her fluffy slippers. She must have changed after I went to bed. (I crawled into bed wearing my clothes.)

I'm so relieved it's Mom that my legs turn to jelly. "Why are you awake?" I ask her. "Is everything okay?"

"Everything is fine," she says, then winces and moves her hand from her chest to the side of her stomach.

"What?" I say.

Mom smiles. "I'm in labor."

37

DON'T PANIC

My brain revs like a race car.
"But Boo's not due yet," I say.

"Well, someone forgot to explain calendars to your sister."

I don't laugh, but Mom does. "Relax. She's early but she'll be fine," she says.

"But Paul's not home."

"Nope," Mom says. "He's not. It's you and me, kiddo."

"Did you call him?"

"Yes. But the storm is bad and the roads are icy."

"He's in a snowplow. Can't he plow through it?"

Mom closes the fridge and opens the freezer instead. "He's way on the other side of town. He'll get here when he can."

"Shouldn't we go to the hospital?"

Mom stops searching the freezer to look at me. "Whoa. Enough with the interrogation already, Mr. Forensic Science Investigator," she teases. "I told you. The roads are bad. Don't panic. We have plenty of time. I was in labor with you for fourteen hours."

Fourteen hours? Okay. Paul should be back by then. My brain eases off the gas.

Mom holds up a box. "Wanna Popsicle?"

"Really? It's the middle of the night."

Mom shrugs. "Why not? I want a Popsicle. And it's not like you have to get up for school in the morning. They called a snow day about an hour ago."

I pump my fist. "Sweet!"

Mom and I end up camping out in Mom and Paul's bedroom. We have Popsicles (cherry for me, raspberry for her) and watch reruns on the small TV on their dresser. It feels reckless, but in a good way. Like when I was younger and Mom and I would run out to the grocery store to get stuff for s'mores on summer nights.

Every once in a while, Mom winces and screws up her face for thirty seconds or so. I wait for it to pass.

"Does it hurt?" I ask.

"I'm okay. No worries." She nudges me with the shoulder closest to mine. "Thank you for keeping me company."

"Will Boo be all right?"

"Yes," she says. "I promise."

I'm not sure how she can promise something like that. But before I can ask, Mom's phone buzzes. She reads it and chuckles. "Wow. Paul is *freaking* out," she tells me. "He says he's willing to call a police escort if need be."

Part of me secretly wishes he would. I'd feel better if he was around to deal with this. At least he's taken a class.

"What are you texting him?" I ask Mom.

"I told him to finish filming the segment. We won't need to head to the hospital until tomorrow," she says. (*Isn't it technically tomorrow?* I think.)

She turns to me. "I don't want him rushing on these roads anyway."

"What about Mrs. Penny?" I ask. Mrs. Penny is our neighbor. She's like ninety years old but always waves to us from her porch. "I could put on my boots and coat and walk to her house. She could drive us to the hospital."

"I swear to you, Felix. There's no rush. I called my doctor earlier and she said it's fine to wait. The contractions are far apart and not regular. Besides, Mrs. Penny can barely drive in good weather."

Mom and I crack up.

We find a movie to watch and settle under a blanket. Three commercial breaks into it, Mom lets out a sound. It's different than the rest I've heard.

I sit straight up.

38

OKAY, PANIC A LITTLE

"Bad contraction?" I ask her, my voice more nervous than I want it to be.

"For the record," Mom says, "there's no such thing as a *good* contraction."

She laughs at her own joke. "No. It's not a contraction," she sighs. "I'm thinking about all the things I wanted to get done before the baby came. Like wash more onesies and put everything away in the dresser. I wish I had more time."

I lean back against the pillow, relieved.

"Oh, well," Mom says. "Can't do anything about it now. Not unless you're up for doing laundry in the middle of the night."

"Pass," I tell her. This gets another laugh, which makes me feel good. At least making Mom laugh is something I can do to help.

"I got the special turtle blanket you picked out for your sister washed, though," Mom says. "Remind me to put it in the hospital bag in the morning. It's hanging on the crib."

I tell her I'll try.

"Oh, shoot. I just realized something else," Mom says. "We're going to have to move our court date to change our names. That's disappointing. I hope we can do it by the end of December. It would be nice to start off the new year with our new name."

I don't know what to say to this, so I say nothing.

Mom's voice turns more serious. "Have you decided if you'd like to change your name, too? Thanks to your sister, we have some extra time."

"I don't know."

Mom considers this. "Want to talk about it? Maybe weigh some pros and cons?"

"No."

"Okay," she says.

"I mean, I've done that already," I lie, because it seems important to her that I've actually considered the pros and cons.

"That's good," Mom says. "Look, I know it's a change. And like Dr. Ryan said, new stuff can be overwhelming. I don't mean to push. I'm only trying to understand how you feel, is all."

Mom has another contraction. We wait it out, her grimacing and me holding her hand. I think about the first time she and Paul brought the name change thing up. "It's a small, little punctuation mark," she'd said.

It doesn't feel small. I wanted to find my dad and talk to him before I had to decide.

That clearly isn't going to happen. So, now what?

Mom releases my hand, letting me know the contraction is over.

"I'd like to understand," she says, like our conversation wasn't interrupted by Boo. I can tell she means it, too.

This might not be the best time, but, to be fair, Mom was the one who brought it up. And who knows when I'll get another chance to talk to her all alone?

"I guess..." I start. And then stop. Mom rubs the top of my hand.

I'm not sure I can explain it right, but I try again because we can do hard things when they're for people we love. Or hope to love.

"I wanted to talk to my dad first," I tell Mom. "To see if he wanted to meet me and maybe get to know me. It's why I took his shirt and wore it at the interview."

Mom frowns. "I see," she says.

"I mean, doesn't he have to give you permission to change my name or something anyway?" I ask her.

Her voice is clear and steady when she speaks. "Well, as a matter of fact, we wouldn't need your dad's permission to change your last name. If that's what you decide."

"But he's my dad. Shouldn't he know?" I drop my gaze.

"Felix," Mom says, pulling my chin up. Her eyes are shiny and I wonder if it's tears or the light from the television playing tricks.

"Buddy...your father hasn't had a legal say in your life since you were a year old."

The "legal say" part makes me think of Casey and how she said her bio-mom sees her but doesn't have any legal rights. What was it Casey said her bio-mom signed? Parental something-or-other?

"Wait. You took away my dad's parental rights?" I ask Mom.

"No," she says gently. "I didn't."

She stays quiet and waits for me to catch up.

She didn't take away his rights. My dad gave them up on his own.

It doesn't matter if I change my last name or not. My dad doesn't want to get to know who I am. It was too late, even before Casey and I started investigating.

He decided for the both of us. When I was just a baby.

Hot tears prick my eyes.

"I'm so sorry," Mom tells me. "Would you like to—" But I don't want to talk anymore. I turn away and snuggle under the blanket. Mom tucks it around me. Or tries to. Boo's in the way.

But by this time tomorrow, Boo will be here. She and Mom and Paul will be the perfect family. I'll just be Mom's other kid. The kid whose dad didn't want him.

The noise and flickering light from the television eventually lull me asleep. As I drift off, I wonder if I'll ever stop feeling like an extra puzzle piece.

My bad dream comes back. This time, I know it's Mom who's moaning. It's loud and eerie. Almost as if...

The first thing I notice when I wake up is that the light in Mom's bathroom is on. Mom's not in bed anymore, so I go over and knock on the door, which is cracked open.

"Ahhhhhhhh, mmmmmm."

"Mom?"

"Felix." Her breathing sounds hard and fast. I open the door all the way. Mom's sitting on the floor, leaning against the side of the bathtub.

"Call 911," she says.

39

"SHE'S COMING!"

*My fingers seem to belong to someone else.
I manage to tap the numbers on Mom's
cell phone anyway.*

"Nine-one-one. What's the address of your emergency?" a woman's voice says.

On TV they always ask *what's* your emergency first. Right? *Right?* I can't remember my address.

Mom moans from the bathroom.

"Hello?" the person on the other end of the phone asks. "What's the address of your emergency?"

I remember it.

"Can I have your name and phone number?" the lady says.

I tell her.

"What's going on, Felix?" the dispatcher wants to know.

I walk back to the bathroom and talk along the way. "My mom's having my baby sister!"

"I want to make sure I'm understanding you correctly, Felix," the dispatcher says. "Your mom is in labor?"

"Yes!"

"Is there anyone else at home right now? Or is it only you and your mom?"

"Paul is supposed to be home but he's at work and got stuck in the snow. He's my stepdad."

"Felix, listen to me, okay?" The dispatcher's voice is calm, which is annoying. Doesn't she get that this is an emergency?

"Can you send an ambulance?" I plead. "I don't know what to do."

Mom is curled up, holding her stomach with both hands. I kneel down next to her.

"An ambulance is already on the way," the dispatcher tells me. "But I'm going to ask you some questions, and I need you to answer them."

Hold on. She's doing Priya's first rule: Assess, then progress. *Okay. I've done this before. I get it.*

"All right," I tell the dispatcher.

"Where is your mom right now?"

"With me. We're in the bathroom. She's on the floor."

"Can you help her to a bed?"

Mom and I struggle to get her standing, since she needs both of my shoulders for support. We shuffle back to her bed.

When I tell the dispatcher, she says, "Good job, Felix. Do you know how old your mom is?"

"I don't remember."

"Can you ask her? Is she able to talk?"

"Mom, how old are you?" I ask, but Mom's face is red and scrunched up in pain. She shakes her head to let me know she can't talk.

"I think she's having a contraction!" I tell the lady on the phone.

"Felix, I need you to remain calm. Now, can you remember how old your mom is? Or *about* how old she is?"

Why does she need to know this, for Pete's sake? "Oh, wait," I say. "I'm eleven and she had me when she was twenty-one. Thirty-two," I tell the dispatcher.

"Thank you. You're doing great. Can your mom talk yet?"

"No, but she's making noise." I hold the phone out so the lady can hear Mom, who's moaning and crying a little now, too.

"Hello? Are you there? Felix?" I pull the phone back.

"I'm here."

"Felix, I need you to stay on the line with me, okay? Help is coming, but your mom and I need you to listen to me and stay calm. Can you do that?"

I nod. "Yes."

"Good. Do you know how many months pregnant your mom is?"

"Nooo." I feel my own tears coming.

"That's okay. Let's figure this out, all right? Do you know when the baby's due?"

"December tenth. She's early. Is she going to be okay?"

"You're doing great. And we're going to do everything we can to make sure your sister is perfectly fine. How's your mom? If she can answer, ask her how far apart the contractions are."

Why isn't the ambulance here yet?

"Mom! They want to know how far apart the contractions are!"

Mom holds up two fingers. Why is she giving me a peace sign? Oh.

"Two minutes," I tell the dispatcher. There are typing sounds coming from the other end.

"Thank you, Felix. Now, I need you to do me a few things. First, go to the front door and unlock it. Okay? That way the paramedics can get in. After that, go find some clean towels and a clean, soft blanket. Then I need you to run back to Mom, got it? Take the phone with you."

I put the phone in the pocket of my sweat pants and head down the hall. The linen closet is on the way, so I grab the towels first and then stop in the middle of the hall. Shoot. Where's the turtle blanket? Mom said something about reminding her to put it in their hospital bag. I close my eyes like Ray does when he wants to remember a crime scene.

The nursery!

The turtle blanket is hanging over the railing of the crib. I grab it and run down the stairs to unlock the front door before darting up again.

"I'm back with my mom," I tell the lady on the phone. "Is the ambulance almost here?"

"They're coming as fast as they can. How's your mom doing?"

Mom's face is red again and she's panting like a dog. It's like the kind of stuff she and Paul used to practice and laugh about when they took that birthing class.

Man. I wish Paul was here now.

I tell the 911 lady what's happening. She tells me to tell Mom not to push.

"Don't push! Don't push!" I say.

Mom lets out a short, sharp cry. "I have to," she says. "*Aaaahhh.* I'm sorry. She's coming!"

40

BOO

"Felix, listen to me. I'm right here and I'm going to stay on the phone with you until help arrives," the dispatcher tells me. *"Things are about to start happening very quickly. I need you to do exactly what I say. Can you do that?"*

"Yes."

"Good."

Mom is crying, and my whole body feels like a knot getting pulled tighter and tighter. If Casey was here, she'd tell me to "gather my Zen," so I try. Only I count to three instead of five on my inhale and exhale. The knot loosens, which is good because the dispatcher is giving me instructions, one right after the other.

"Help Mom get into a comfortable position using pillows or rolled-up blankets."

"Spread the clean towels under your mom's bottom."

"Remind your mom to breathe."

Mom keeps saying, "I'm so sorry, baby. I'm so sorry. I know this is scary." I'm not sure if she's talking to me or to Boo.

I pat her shoulder and tell her it's going to be okay (because the lady on the phone told me to do that, too).

"Is the baby crowning? Can you see her head?" the dispatcher asks.

"I don't know," I tell her. "I'm not, um, down there."

Mom reaches between her legs. "I can feel her!"

"You're doing great, ma'am," I hear the lady say loudly. "Felix?"

"Yeah?"

"Tell your mom to push on the next contraction if she feels the need to."

I tell her.

"Aaaaaaaaaaahhhhh."

The lady in my ear says, *"Push, one, two, three..."* I start counting out loud along with her.

"Remind Mom to breathe, Felix."

"Breathe, Mom! Why isn't the ambulance here?"

"It's coming, Felix," the dispatcher says. "They're almost there. Focus on your mom for me."

Mom has two more contractions. The three of us are in the middle of doing our *push, one, two, three...* thing when suddenly Mom's face changes. She looks surprised.

"Catch her!" Mom yells at me.

I move in front of Mom's legs. And holy cow, Boo is out! She looks gross and slimy; she's kind of purple and covered in blood and white gunk. But I reach out and hold her under her back anyway.

I can finally hear an ambulance siren in the distance.

"Felix? Felix?" I hear the dispatcher say. I didn't even know I'd dropped the phone on the bed. "Is the baby out?"

"Yes!" I report. Mom picks up the phone and puts it on speaker for us.

"Good," the dispatcher says. "Now let's make sure she's breathing. Take one of the towels you got and gently clean off her face. Be careful not to rub too hard, though."

Mom leans forward as best she can. "Is she okay? Is she breathing?"

I do what the dispatcher told me, but it's hard because Boo is slippery. And she's so tiny! I don't want to hurt her. Her face scrunches up and gets red.

"Waaaaaah!"

Man, she looks mad. But she's making a noise and that must be good because everyone starts laughing. Mom, me, the lady on the phone. I think we're all relieved.

The siren outside is closer.

"Excellent job, Felix," the dispatcher tells me. "The paramedics just turned onto your street. You have one last job, okay? I want you to wrap the baby up in the blanket you got earlier. Cover her head, too. But not her face. Understand?"

"What about the cord?" I ask.

"Don't worry about that. The paramedics will take care of it."

"Hand her to me, Felix," Mom says. She looks exhausted.

I carefully scoop up Boo and lay her on the turtle blanket so I can wrap her up like a burrito, like the mom at the baby doctor's office showed me.

It seems like proper introductions are in order. "Hey there," I say. "I'm your big brother, Felix."

"Is she okay?" Mom says from the head of the bed. "Does she have her fingers and toes?"

I look. She does.

And guess what? That's not all she has.

Boo is a boy!

41

THE FOUR OF US

As soon as I lay Boo on Mom's chest, the
paramedics come through the front door.
The dispatcher tells me again that I did a great job.
I say thanks, and then we hang up. It feels weird,
like we've become best friends or something.

You'd think everyone would move at lightning speed, but the paramedics seem relaxed. Mom is smiling as they examine her and the baby. I stand off in the corner, out of the way. One of the paramedics comes over, pats me on the back, and says if he's not careful, I'll be taking over his job soon.

And then he says, "Why don't you go get some shoes and a coat on? You can ride in the ambulance with your mom and brother."

Brother.

How weird is that? Boo is a boy. A BOY.

Mom keeps grinning and saying, "I can't believe it."

I wonder how Paul will react.

When we get to the hospital, they put me in the hallway by the nurses' station. I guess they think I'm too young to be left alone in the waiting room.

Paul comes running in five minutes after we get there. His cameraman, Matt, follows behind.

When Paul sees me, he grabs me in a big bear hug. The awkwardness that has been between us for the last week is gone, squeezed out when he accidentally almost breaks a rib.

Paul pulls back to look me in the face. "Felix! Are you okay? Is your mom okay? Where is she?"

"I'm good," I tell him. "Mom's down there." I thrust my thumb down the hall. A nurse comes over and tells Paul to follow her.

It's just me and Matt now. He offers to walk me down to the hospital food court to get breakfast, even though it's still mostly dark.

"I can't believe how hungry I am," I tell Matt on the way.

He laughs. "Medical emergencies can do that. It's the adrenaline. You'll probably crash later."

Over two orders of biscuits and gravy, Matt tells me how he and Paul got the call about Mom having the baby when they were almost home. (One of the paramedics called him from the ambulance.) "We changed directions and headed straight here," Matt says.

He wants to know how it happened, so I tell him the whole story.

"No way," Matt says when I get to the end and reveal that Boo is a boy instead of a girl. "Man," he says, "that's awesome."

Matt walks me back upstairs and asks me to give Paul the message that he'll check in later. One of the nurses takes me to Mom's room. "It's not visiting hours," she says. "But seeing as you're a hero, I think we can make an exception."

Mom is snoring quietly in her hospital bed.

Paul motions me over to the rocking chair, where he's holding the baby, who is also sound asleep. "I can't get over how small he is," Paul whispers. "I mean, look at that nose. Have you ever seen such a tiny nose?"

Boo (do I still call him that?) is wearing a blue-and-pink-striped hat that looks like it would fit a doll. But I can see a bit of hair sticking out from underneath. His hair is dark, like mine. He's *a lot* cuter than the last time I saw him.

"I can't believe he's actually here," Paul says.

"I can't believe he's a he," I say.

Paul chuckles. "I know, right? Your mom and I are freaking out about that. The doctor told us ultrasounds can be wrong sometimes. Especially when the prediction is for a girl. Things can hide sometimes. If you know what I mean." (I do.)

Paul asks me if I want to hold the baby.

My brother looks warm and content in Paul's arms. Plus, I feel bad for Paul that he didn't get to be first.

"Later," I tell him.

Paul yawns and that makes me yawn. He gently puts the baby in the clear bassinet that's next to Mom's bed.

"We should follow your mom's lead and get some sleep while we can," he whispers. "I'll take the rocker if you want the bench by the window."

When I get to the window, I peek outside. This part of the hospital faces a big field. The snow on the ground is my favorite kind—a giant, blank piece of paper waiting to be written on.

I don't feel tired, but there's nothing to do, so I stretch out on the bench with the blanket and pillow the nurses brought.

"What a crazy night, huh?" Paul whispers a few minutes later.

"Crazy," I agree.

"Felix? Thank you for being there for your mom and the baby. I'm sorry I couldn't get home in time."

I feel a pang. Even after everything I did, Paul is apologizing to *me*.

"It's okay," I tell him. "You're here now."

I know Paul's smiling even though I can't see him.

"Still," he says. "I'm grateful." He's quiet for a while and I think maybe he's fallen asleep. But then he speaks again. "You, your mom, and your brother mean the world to me. You know that, right?"

The rocker makes a rhythmic squeak.

"Yeah," I say. Or at least I think I say it. I'm suddenly so tired that I'm not sure the signal went from my brain to my mouth. The room is quiet, and I can hear everyone breathing or snoring or making tiny mouse sounds from the bassinet. I realize something.

"Paul?"

"Hmmmmm?" he says.

I want to point out that this is the first time we're all together. The four of us. It doesn't feel like there are stepsomethings or half somethings. Just one whole family. But the sun has shifted higher in the sky, shining through the crack in the curtains and getting in my face, so I shut my eyes and listen to the rocker going back and forth, back and forth, back and

42

BABY NAMES

Around six o'clock that night, Matt and his wife
show up at the hospital with a Hawaiian pizza,
blue balloons, and presents in tow. The five of us
have a picnic right there in Mom's room while
the baby is down in the nursery. They're keeping a
close eye on him, since he was three weeks early.

Matt's wife asks me about my 911 call. Christy thinks what happened would make a great story for her newspaper. I wonder out loud if it's really that interesting.

"Are you kidding?" Mom says. "You did an amazing thing. You helped deliver your baby brother in the middle of a snowstorm. How many kids your age can say that?"

Mom turns to Christy. "The nurses even made him his own hero's medal," she says. "Felix, show her."

I retrieve the medal—if you can call it that—from the nearby table. When the night nurses heard that I'd helped deliver my brother, they cut out a cardboard star and covered it in aluminum foil. They added "ribbons" made out of pieces of gauze and medical tape. I think they made it because they thought I was younger than I really am, but I thanked them anyway when they presented it to me this morning.

"It's up to you," Christy tells me. "I'd love to do the story, but I won't if you're not one hundred percent on board."

A story about me delivering my brother isn't the same as a feature about the Forensic Science Club tournament. But who knows? Maybe the result will be the same. My dad could see it and change his mind. I tell Christy I'm game.

Ten minutes later, the nurse pops her head in, rolling a bassinet along with her. "Sorry to interrupt the party, but someone is getting fussy."

The nurse kicks Matt and Christy out, saying nonfamily visiting hours are over. She lets Christy snap a quick picture of me with the baby first.

"He must be hungry," Paul says. I am, too. I wander down to the nurses' station, where there's a cart with snacks and mini-size sodas and juice boxes for families in the maternity ward. There are only a few people around. I overhear the nurses talking about the snow. Apparently, they're short-staffed since schools were closed.

I wonder what Ray, Priya, and Casey are doing with their snow day. Is everyone still mad at me for getting us disqualified yesterday?

Yesterday. Wow. I can't believe it's barely been twenty-four hours. Helping Mom deliver the baby. Coming to the hospital. The world covered in white outside. The hushed halls inside. Everything feels like a cross between being awake and asleep, like the storm dropped a spell on us along with the snow.

Paul would let me use his phone to message my friends, since I left mine at home. But I'm not even sure what I'd say.

Ray won't get the chance to show his dad that Forensic Science Club isn't a waste of time. Priya's friends will keep thinking it's weird she likes crimes and dead bodies. Casey won't get her own trophy and the spotlight for a change.

I'm getting my newspaper story, though. It doesn't feel right. *I* was the one who messed up. I could tell Christy I've changed my mind, but Mom and Paul would want to know why. I'd have to tell them about cheating. And that would break the spell. I'm not ready for that.

When I get back to the room, the baby is fussing. Paul is doing the sway-and-bounce technique with him. At least that's what Mom's calling it. Whatever it is, it's not working very well. I must look amused because Paul says, "You think it's easy? Here, you give it a shot."

"Wash your hands first," Mom tells me.

After finishing up at the sink, I sit down in the rocker and get a lecture from Mom about supporting the baby's head and putting this hand here and putting the other one there, but I got it. The second he's settled in my arms, my brother stops fussing.

"How'd you do that?" Paul asks.

I shrug. "Guess he likes me." As if to prove I'm right, the baby grabs my finger.

"You're hired," Mom says. "I'll let the school know you're dropping out to be a full-time baby whisperer."

The three of us laugh. It feels good. Like I'm one of the grown-ups this time, instead of the smallest person in the room.

Before Matt and Christy left, Christy handed Mom a gift bag and said, "Something to keep you three occupied tonight. You know, in case you weren't busy enough."

It turns out it was a baby name book.

Mom groans, but in a playful way. "Okay. We gotta rethink more than the pink clothes. What are we going to name this little guy?"

Paul thumbs through the book, throwing out a ton of names. None of them seem to suit the baby.

"We could name him after his dad," Mom suggests. Paul nixes that idea immediately.

"I'm not a fan of juniors," he says.

"Hunter still works," Mom offers.

"True," Paul says. "What do you think, Felix?"

I study my brother's face. "I don't know. He doesn't look like a Hunter to me."

"What are we going to do?" Mom says, exasperated. "We can't keep calling him Boo."

Paul snaps his fingers. "I got it." Satisfaction spreads across his face. "I know exactly what we should do."

"Well, go on," Mom says. "Don't keep us in suspense."

Paul looks right at me. "I think you should choose the name, Felix. After all, you were the one who helped deliver him."

Mom looks as surprised as I feel. But she lets the idea sink in for a minute.

"I think," she says slowly, "that's a great idea. It'll be our gift to you for coming through for me and your brother. Oh, wow. I can't get used to saying that. I've got two sons." She smiles.

"Hold on," I say. "You're letting *me* pick the baby's name?"

"Sure," Paul says. "Why not?"

The emotions of last week come flooding back. "I don't deserve to," I tell him. "Not after what I did to your chest."

"I know you're sorry about that, kiddo," Paul says.

"And for lying about it," I manage to get past the lump in my throat.

"And for that, too," he says. "Water under the bridge. Showing up when things get tough and taking responsibility for mistakes are signs of maturity. I'm proud of you."

"Thanks," I say.

"You're going to be a great big brother," Paul says.

"How can you tell? I mean besides that I'm kind of a baby whisperer."

Mom and Paul laugh. But then Paul grows serious. "Because you're already a great son."

Like Casey, I'm a balloon. Only instead of being filled with too much air, I'm filled with helium.

"You're really letting me pick out the name?"

"Yes," Mom says. "Nothing crazy, like something from a video game, though," she warns me. "I reserve the right to veto."

I look down. The baby's eyes are slits of gray and he's doing this cute thing with his mouth, as if he's sucking on his own tongue. His head smells like warm bread.

"So, what does he look like?" Paul asks.

"I'm not sure yet," I tell him.

Whatever I pick has to go with Fine-Woods. David or Ethan, maybe? Or a name that starts with *F*, like mine. Franklin? Forrest? Okay, definitely not Forrest. Forrest plus Woods would be too many tree references.

I lean my face closer to the baby and whisper, "What should I name you?"

And just like that, I realize I already know.

43

LOCARD WAS RIGHT

*Paul lets me skip school on Friday to catch up on
sleep and help him get things ready at the house
for Mom and the baby. "It's one more day," he says.
"You're not going to miss much."*

Playing hooky is fine by me. What if Ray tells me we're not
friends anymore, like Casey did? I don't know how I'm going to
face either of them or Priya. Or Mr. S, for that matter.

Paul and I spend the morning cleaning and doing laundry. After washing all the sheets and blankets from Mom and
Paul's bed (last night, Paul slept on the couch), the two of us
head back to the hospital.

Halfway there, my phone pings. Mr. S sent me an email,
asking me to stop by his room during my study hall on Monday. I hope I'm not getting kicked out of Forensic Science Club.

I chew the edge of my thumbnail. Paul notices but doesn't
say anything. I know I should tell him and Mom what happened. And not because Mr. S might call them.

"Hey, Paul?"

"Yeah?"

"Something happened and I need help trying to figure out how to fix it."

"Sure," Paul says. "I'll do my best."

I tell Paul about cheating during the last crime scene. I tell him why it was important to win and to get in the newspaper. I'm worried that the truth—that I was looking for my dad— might hurt his feelings. But I remember what Paul said about taking responsibility.

I finish spilling everything to Paul as he pulls into the hospital parking lot. He kills the engine and turns around to look at me.

"First of all, I want you to know that I understand why you're curious about your dad. I would be, too, if I were you. I promise not to take it personally. And whatever you and your mom want to do, I'm on board.

"As far as the cheating goes," he says, "all I can tell you is that, from my experience, honesty will go a long way in getting you respect and forgiveness in this world."

"Thanks," I tell him.

"No problem. Know what you're going to do?"

"Nope."

"That's okay. You'll figure it out."

The two of us climb out of the car and head into the hospital. While we're waiting for the elevator, Paul turns to me and says, "You good?"

"Yeah. I think so."

Paul grins. "Glad to hear it. Because if you weren't, I was going to tell you my new vegetable joke."

"Vegetable joke?"

"Yeah," Paul says. "It's corny."

Mom is craving an Italian sub sandwich, so Paul goes down to the hospital food court. I ask him to bring me back some biscuits and gravy.

The baby is asleep in his bassinet. Mom must have known the baby burrito trick because he's wrapped up tight. I plop down in the rocking chair and check out the haul of baby gifts sitting on a table. I guess people give presents before the baby comes *and* after. It's mostly flowers and teddy bears holding plastic balloons. But there's a bottle of sparkling grape juice, too. We're going to need a box to bring everything home.

"Those are pretty," I say, motioning toward a vase of yellow roses.

"Aren't they?" Mom replies. "Paul's parents sent them. They..."

She pauses.

"They what?" I ask, wondering if she's lost her train of thought. That happens to me when I haven't gotten enough sleep.

Mom holds my gaze. "They remind me of the flowers your dad brought when you were born."

My brain and mouth both forget how to work for a few seconds.

"Uh...*what?*" I manage.

Her voice trembles, but she doesn't look away. "They remind me of the flowers your dad brought to the hospital the day you were born."

Like she did the other night, Mom waits for me to catch up. It doesn't take long.

"My dad was there when I was born?" I ask.

Mom nods. "Yes. He said he thought you looked like me. Which he said was a good thing because I was way better-looking than he was." She smiles at the memory.

"I don't understand," I say. "I thought..."

Well, for the record, I'm not sure what I thought.

"Oh, boy," Mom tells me. "He bought these blue gum cigars and handed them out. And he took a bunch of pictures of you. He loved rocking you, and thought you looked really sweet when you were sleeping. He said he was going to go out and get a tattoo of your birth date. Which was funny considering he was terrified of needles."

Mom looks right at me. "Felix, your dad was so proud when you were born. You should know that."

I take a minute to let this sink in. The curtains are open, and the field of snow outside is even bigger than it looked before. Someone has walked through it and left long, wandering tracks.

When I look back, Mom is waiting.

"But why didn't he stick around?" I ask. "And why did he sign away his rights?"

"I don't know," she says. "Like I said, I don't think he was ready to be a dad. He loved—loves—you, though. That I know."

"How can you love someone and leave?"

"Fair question," she tells me. "I guess it's complicated."

"That's not a good answer."

"No," Mom says. "I suppose it's not."

"Why didn't you tell me any of this?" I ask.

"I meant to," she says. "But the first time you asked about your dad, I thought you were too young. So I put it off. I told myself it wasn't a big deal; you were a preschooler, you'd forget. I figured

I'd get around to having a conversation with you eventually. But when you asked again, I decided 'not today.' And then 'not today' eventually became a habit. It felt safer. Does that make any sense?"

"Yeah, I guess," I tell her.

I try to sort this new information in my head, adding it to things I already know. My dad's name is Michael but he goes by Mikey. He's short, like me, and he played flag football in college. He had a dog. He bought gum cigars when I was born. He's terrified of needles.

And—this is the big one—he was there when I was born. He held me.

"Felix," Mom says, drawing me out of my own thoughts. "I was wrong and I owe you an apology. I'm not happy that you wore your dad's T-shirt for the interview and lied about the chest. But it made me realize how important knowing about your dad is to you. I wasn't ready to see that."

The baby cries in his sleep. Mom rocks his bassinet and he settles down quickly.

"And, if I'm being perfectly honest," Mom says softly, "I wasn't ready to deal with it, either."

"But you are now?"

"It doesn't matter if I am or not. *You're* ready."

Mom pats an open space next to her on the bed, and I climb up. "I don't know where your father is at the moment," she says. "Last I heard, he lived on the West Coast."

I feel sucker-punched. My dad doesn't live in his hometown— or even in Ohio—anymore. The television interview, the newspaper article about the tournament. I never had a shot to begin with.

Mom goes on. "But I know people who can get in touch with him. We can do that, if you'd like, and see where it takes us. How would you feel about that?"

"I'm not sure," I tell her. "It's complicated."

She laughs. "Fair."

Mom pushes aside my bangs. "I have a few pages from your baby book you should probably see."

She drops her hand when she sees my expression.

"I tore them out after your dad left. It's not my proudest moment," she admits. "I put them away in case . . . well . . . in case you ever wanted them." She pauses, collecting herself. "If you'd like, I have some photos of your dad, too. You look a lot like him."

I know I do. But I decide to keep the photo I found in the buffet to myself.

Paul comes waltzing in, loaded down with bags from three different food places. "Lunch is served," he says. "Now, no complaints. I spent all day hunting and foraging for these nourishing meals."

"Nourishing I'm not so sure about," Mom says. "But who cares? I just birthed a human and I'm starving."

I hop down from the bed. Paul insists I take the rocker and he sits on the bench. As we eat, Mom and Paul talk about checking out and how Paul will have to get the car seat installed so it can pass the hospital's inspection before Mom and the baby can leave.

But I'm not really paying attention. I'm thinking about everything Mom told me about my dad, and about Locard's exchange principle. Locard was right. We take and leave pieces of ourselves wherever we go.

Even if we don't know it.

44

FORGIVEN

Mom and the baby came home on Saturday.
Things haven't been bad. The baby cries but he's
not very loud. He sleeps a lot, too. Mom assures
me this is the "honeymoon phase."

"He's resting up from the delivery," she said. "Soon he'll discover how powerful his lungs are."

Paul offers to drive me to school, since he's on paternity leave. It's Monday. My first day back since the disaster that was the final crime scene. We're running late, which means we have to walk in together to sign the late arrival log. In the "reason for tardy" box, Paul writes: *NEW BABY!* I'm surprised he's not carrying around a sign. He even told a random mom in the school parking lot. It's embarrassing, but also funny.

Ms. Markson, the school secretary, is on the phone. She holds up her hand for us to wait. After she hangs up, she stands. "Congratulations," she says, drawing it out into a dozen syllables. "A new baby!"

She turns to me. "And a bona fide hero!"

Ms. Good, the principal, and Mr. Farley, the vice-principal, come out of their offices to join the fuss.

Ms. Markson grabs the newspaper from the counter and shows it to us. We've already seen it. And we have several copies.

The article that Christy wrote came out on Saturday. It was on the front page of the metro section and included the picture Christy took of me and the baby in the hospital.

The headline reads: *Eleven-Year-Old Helps Deliver Brother in Snowstorm.*

Christy described what happened and how I responded. She even tracked down the 911 dispatcher, whose name, it turns out, was Diane. She said, "Felix did an amazing job keeping calm in a very stressful situation." (I'm not sure about the keeping calm part.)

Ms. Good pats me on the back. "Well done, Felix. You're a wonderful representative of our school."

It's not the last pat on the back I get. All morning, people stop me to say "Way to go!" and "Nice job." A couple of people ask me if it was gross watching a baby being born, but I tell them it wasn't that bad.

Instead of going to study hall, I head to Mr. S's biology room. His class is working, so the two of us step out into the hallway.

"Thanks for meeting me," Mr. S says. "I'll make this quick."

My whole body tenses.

"First, congrats on the neonate."

I draw a blank. Mr. S smiles. "I mean the baby, your new brother."

"Oh. Thank you."

Mr. S looks me in the eye. "Second, I wanted to make sure that what happened last week won't happen again. Cheating is serious."

"I know," I say. "It won't."

He nods once. "Good. That's all I needed to hear." Now that I know I'm not being kicked out of the club, I relax.

Mr. S's expression softens. "How's your team taking it?"

"They weren't happy," I admit.

Mr. S gives me a sympathetic look. "I bet they'll come around. Let's step inside and I'll write you a late pass." He turns toward the door.

When I don't move, he looks back. "Something else on your mind?" he asks.

"I have an idea."

I don't run into Ray or Casey, but I see Priya since the two of us share the same lunch period. Her friends pretend not to be listening when I sit down next to her at their table and start talking. There are only a few minutes until the bell rings.

"Hey," I say.

"Hey yourself," she says.

"Are you still mad?"

Priya considers this. "Not really. I mean, I was. But I'm not anymore. I figured you probably had a good reason."

"I thought I did."

Priya nods. "I understand." She lowers her voice and leans closer. "I cheated once. Totally got caught, too."

"You did?"

Priya leans back. "Don't act so surprised. I'm not perfect. And I'm not proud of it or anything. But I get it. It sucks that the rest of us have to suffer the consequences, though."

"I think I found a way to make things better with Ray, at least."

"That's good."

"I wish there was a way I could make it up to you and Casey, too."

Priya waves me off. "I can't speak for Casey, but you could tell me about the 911 call and being in the ambulance sometime. I don't need the gory details. Just the basics about procedures. That stuff is fascinating."

One of Priya's friends scoffs when Priya says "fascinating." But Priya ignores her.

I hold out my hand for her to shake. "Deal."

The Forensic Science Club is having a party to celebrate the end of the session. Mr. S says he's going to try to keep the club running for spring semester. Everyone cheers. Maybe there'll be another chance for my team to go a tournament. And another shot for Paul to solve a crime scene for parents.

Priya, Ray, and I are sitting at our table. We're eating cupcakes with shards of fake glass sticking out of the top, drizzled with fake blood. There are homemade pretzels shaped to look like bones and thumbprint cookies with real thumbprints on them, too.

Casey is at another table, talking to another team, and doing a great job ignoring me.

I'm surprised that Ray is here. But I'm not complaining. Now I have a chance to tell him what Mr. S and I talked about.

Priya keeps giving me a look and tilting her head in Ray's direction, trying to get me to talk. I take a breath and give it a shot.

"Did you get my texts?" I ask Ray. (I sent a few over the weekend.)

"Yeah," he says. "I didn't feel like talking."

I glance at Priya. She gives another look that says *Keep going!*

"How about now?" I ask Ray.

He looks at me. "I don't know about talking, but I wouldn't mind if you want to apologize some more."

"I apologize some more," I say.

Ray pulls a shard of sugar glass out of his cupcake and licks off the fake blood. "Okay," he says. "Now I wouldn't mind some groveling." He's smirking.

"Come on, you two," Priya says. "Patch things up already. You're friends and we're supposed to be celebrating."

Priya's right. Ray's my friend. And there's a lot I should tell him. Like why I cheated. And about the growth hormone shots, too. But that can wait until later.

"Instead of groveling," I ask Ray, "how about something else?"

He doesn't say anything, but he's curious. I tell him how I asked Mr. S if the club could use a new crime scene diorama.

"I thought you and I could make one together," I say.

Ray grins. "That would be cool. Okay. You're forgiven."

"Finally," Priya says.

"When do you want to do that?" Ray asks.

"I'm not sure," I tell him. "Things are crazy around my house."

"Yeah. I heard about that. You're a big hero celebrity now. You know what that means, right?"

I shake my head.

Ray puts on his serious face. "It means I'm proud of you, Felix."

The two of us crack up while Priya rolls her eyes at us. "Boys are weird," she tell us.

"I agree," Casey says.

45

PEACE OFFERING

*Nobody had noticed Casey standing next to the
table, her shoulders pulled back.*

Priya looks at Ray. "Let's go get more severed-finger cookies.
Wow. There's something I never thought I'd say."

The two of them go, leaving me and Casey alone. I
rehearsed what I wanted to say to her a hundred times and I
can't remember any of it.

We look at each other in silence. Finally, I ask, "So. How
was *your* snow day?"

"Not as interesting as yours," she says. It's not much, but
it's a start.

Casey sits down on the stool across from me and nibbles
on popcorn from inside a plastic baggie with an EVIDENCE
sticker on it. At least she isn't running in the other direction.

"I read that you got a brother," she says. "My brother was
supposed to be a girl, too. Remember?"

"Oh, right!"

There's more awkward silence while everyone around us is laughing and talking and eating freaky-looking food.

And then Casey says, "I like his name. It's a whole lot better than Boo."

"Thanks."

Casey drops a piece of popcorn, picks it up off the table, and examines it like it's evidence.

"Hold on. I have something for you," I tell her, and grab my backpack off the floor.

She stares at what I've handed her. "I give up. What is this?"

"A medal," I tell her. "The nurses made it for me for being a hero."

She raises an eyebrow.

"Yeah, it's kind of silly," I admit. "Anyway, it's not a trophy but . . . I dunno. I thought it could be a peace offering."

When Casey doesn't say anything, I press on. "I'm sorry for cheating and costing you and everyone else a chance to go the tournament."

"I really wanted to go," Casey says.

"I know," I tell her. "And I really wanted to help you. Like you helped me with looking for my dad."

Casey grows quiet again for a bit while she studies the medal.

"Look," she says. "I had every right to be angry at you. I'm not saying I didn't. But that afternoon, my dads got tied up at work and my bio-mom picked me up after the last crime scene. It got me thinking about your plan to get into the newspaper so your dad could find you."

She pauses and lets out a long sigh. "What I'm trying to say is, I get why you felt you needed to cheat. It must be hard for you not to know your biological dad."

"Yeah," I admit. "But I shouldn't have done what I did. Especially because it hurt other people, too."

"I'm sorry we couldn't find him," Casey says.

"It's okay," I tell her. "And actually I have to catch you up on that."

"Oh?"

"Yeah. But maybe now is not the time," I say.

Casey nods. "Here," she says, and hands me the baggie of popcorn. She stands up and gets tape from a nearby shelf. Then she attaches the aluminum-foil star to the front of her hoodie.

"Does this mean—?" I ask.

"We're good. Still friends. Besides, my pops says that missing the tournament will eventually be a small bump on the road of life." Casey pauses and gives a sly smile. "Pops tends to be 'look at the big picture' about things," she explains.

"It could be worse. He could tell dad jokes like Paul," I say.

"Oh, he does that, too. Both my dads do. It's double the agony." Casey and I laugh.

There's another lull. "Do you think he's right about the tournament?" I ask her.

Casey shrugs. "Who knows? The tournament feels like a big deal now. Then again, over the summer, I thought it was a big deal that my brother got sick and we had to skip our annual family trip to Cedar Point. And I got over it." She pauses. "What do you think?"

I turn the question over in my head.

"I think that happens a lot," I say. "I remember one time

my mom grounded me and I was so mad at her that I tried to run away to my neighbor's house. I packed my suitcase with pajamas and snacks and left a note that said she was the meanest mom in the world."

Casey snickers.

"Hey. I was *six*," I tell her. "I can't even remember why I got grounded in the first place. And last Christmas I really wanted this new video game. I spent months begging for it. And now it's under my bed."

Casey nods, but before she can say anything else, Ray and Priya wander over.

"Is it safe to come back yet?" Ray asks.

"It's safe," Casey tells them, and the two of us abandon our conversation.

"Bomb diggity," Priya says. "Because I scored us more evidence." She holds up four baggies with Rice Krispie treats made to look like eyeballs.

We all laugh. Like we're a team again.

"Hey," I ask them. "Do you wanna hear how you helped me deliver my brother?"

46

NOTHING IS LITTLE

*Our neighbor Mrs. Penny brings over a lasagna and
a loaf of garlic bread at dinnertime for me, Mom,
and Paul. After we eat, the three of us—no, I mean
the four of us—hang out in the living room. The
baby sleeps in his bassinet. Mom, Paul, and I stretch
out on the couch and love seat to watch TV.*

Mom keeps yawning.

"Why don't you go to bed, honey?" Paul says to her. "You
need your rest. I'll stay up and bring you the baby when it's
time for him to nurse."

Paul's constantly offering to help with the baby. I wonder how Mom managed alone when I was a newborn. Earlier, when the two of us were changing the baby, she told me
my dad moved away when I was three weeks old for a job in
another state. He'd left money and an address. But Mom was
angry and she didn't keep in touch. Like she promised at
the hospital, she gave me the missing baby book pages and
some photos. A few are of my mom and dad together. Others
are just him. There's even one picture of him holding me in

the hospital. My dad looks happy and scared at the same time. Like he's afraid I might break.

"Was it hard?" I asked her.

"Yes," Mom said. "But I had your grandparents around back then to help, so we managed. Your grandparents were over-the-moon in love with you."

I bet Paul's parents will be like that, too. They've called like five times already. They're coming tomorrow to stay a week and help.

"You should get to bed, too, Felix," Paul tells me, drawing me back to the present.

"Wait," Mom says, sitting up. "Your shot."

I grab the medicine pen from the refrigerator and get it ready. After I bring it out to the living room, Mom cleans my arm with an alcohol pad and pinches it. "All set?" I tell her to go for it. "On the count of three," Mom says. "One, two . . ."

She inspects my arm when she's done. "Oh, no. You're bleeding."

"It's nothing. It's barely bleeding," I tell Mom, but she starts to sniffle anyway.

Paul wraps his arm around her shoulder. He looks at me over her head and mouths, *Hormones.*

Still? I thought once the baby came that would be it. Guess I was wrong.

I get up and get a Band-Aid. I don't really need one, but it's a small thing that'll make Mom feel better.

I've been thinking a lot about small things since my conversation with Casey. And how we don't always know what's going to turn out to be important. Casey asked me if I thought things that seem big can turn out to be small. And I do. But I think the opposite is also true. Sometimes, things that seem small or ordinary in the moment turn out to be big. Like a baseball game. A question. A hyphen. A decision. A conversation. An inch.

They're like bits of trace evidence. You have to see and measure them first.

"What time do your folks get in tomorrow?" Mom is asking Paul.

"Four, I think," he tells her. The baby fusses. Paul starts to haul himself off the couch. "I'll get him."

"Let me," I say, getting up. I lean over the bassinet and coo, "It's okay, little dude." My brother stops making noise when he hears my voice. "Hey, Cole. Did you hear? Grandma and Grandpa are coming tomorrow."

I don't have to look to know that Paul is beaming. When I told him what name I picked out, he was so happy, he cried. Mom did, too.

I scoop my brother up, careful to not let his head flop and to keep my arm firmly underneath his back.

"We should get a family picture taken," I say when we sit down. Mom and Paul exchange a look over my head. I hear Mom sniff. Between the hormones and lack of sleep, Mom is very emotional lately. I think I'll wait to ask her about contacting the lawyer for me to change my last name until she's less weepy.

"Man," Paul says, looking down at Cole. "It's hard to believe one little person can change everything."

I kiss my brother's head.

"Nah," I say. "Not really."

A NOTE FOR MY SHORT READERS

Dear friends,

Like Felix, my daughter was diagnosed with growth hormone deficiency when she was in middle school. Many of the things Felix endures, like the shots and medical tests, are things my daughter also went through. But everyone's experiences are different.

Besides growth hormone deficiency, there are many different kinds of growth disorders or conditions that can make you short. What's most important for you to know is this: Not everyone who is short has a growth disorder. In fact, chances are very good you don't have one. Some people are just meant to be short. Like Felix says, "Somebody has to be at the bottom of the growth charts." This is usually because your parents are on the short side, too. You also might be a late bloomer. This means you simply haven't started to grow yet.

Kids with growth hormone deficiency either are missing the hormone that makes them grow or aren't producing enough of it for a reason. Growth hormone shots replace that missing hormone. Getting shots is like taking insulin if you're diabetic, or even wearing glasses. There's nothing wrong with you; your body just needs help to work properly. Getting shots won't make you grow any taller than you would have if your body made enough hormones. *Some people get shots for the rest of their lives to help their bones and organs. But most people don't have to.*

When it comes to growth disorders, sometimes parents and doctors know right away that there's a problem. Maybe a baby or toddler is tiny or they're not meeting developmental milestones or have other medical issues. Other times, a child grows fine and then that growth starts to slow down. Like I said, everyone's experience is different. If you're shorter than other kids your age, your doctor and the grown-ups you live with are probably aware and on top of things. But if you're worried about it, you can talk to them, too. It's your body. You have a right to know what's going on with it.

I'm one of those people who was meant to be on the short side. When I was young, my nickname was Shorty, so I know there are a lot of cool things about being the short kid. I also know there can be not-so-fun things about it. If you're experiencing some of these things (for example, someone is teasing you or being mean or you're feeling self-conscious), I want to say two things. First, I'm sorry that's happening to you. Second, please talk to an adult you trust about what's going on. They can help.

And one last thing. If you've been diagnosed with growth hormone deficiency or another growth disorder, here's a high five! I hope you enjoy reading about a kid like you. Never let anyone underestimate you.

Your friend,
Shorty

PS. If you'd like more information about growth disorders, you or your grown-ups can visit the MAGIC Foundation at www.MagicFoundation.org.

ACKNOWLEDGMENTS

More than any of my other books to date, this story has been through the wringer. Title, plot, premise—you name it, I've probably changed it. But through it all, my main character has stayed the same. And so has the heart of the story—family. These are the people who've helped me remember that no writer does this alone.

To my editor, Sally Morgridge: I'm thrilled we got to work together again. Thank you for seeing past the clutter and helping me polish my work into something worthy to go into readers' hands. You make me a better writer, and I deeply appreciate your patience and support as this book has evolved over the last few years. And thank you to the rest of the crew at Holiday House, and to Erwin Madrid for the gorgeous cover!

To my agent extraordinaire, Marie Lamba: Knowing I'm in such kind and capable hands makes my job so much easier. Thank you for helping me make my dreams come true and for always being there for me.

To my brilliant critique partners, Kate Fall, Christina Farley, Susan Laidlaw, Andrea Mack, and Debbie Ridpath Ohi:

You've all been on this journey with me from the start and I'm grateful for that every day.

Thank you to all the many Ohio writers whose company and support over the years make me feel like I've been invited to the cool kids' table. Especially: Margaret Peterson Haddix, Jody Casella, Mindy McGinnis, Natalie Richards, Nancy Roe Pimm (my favorite NY conference partner in crime), Mary Kay Carson, Brandon Marie Miller, Michelle Houts, Linda Stanek, and Julie Rubini.

To Stephanie Bunce and Diane Bailey: Thank you for the marathon Panera lunches. The brownies are good but the company is better. To Becka Mette: Thanks for the *Stars Wars* line and for being cool with me complaining about life or writing twice a week for the last ten years. Thank you also to Steve Mette for answering last-minute crime scene procedure questions. And thanks to librarian Kelly Silwani, who helped me track down information about Orange High School's new mascot. (Any errors are the result of the book's going to print before all the information was available.)

To my "little" brothers, Darrell and Mark: It's not fair you guys got all the height, but you're still cool.

In memory of Ricky Walker: Thank you for your insight into what it was like to be a short boy. I'm sad that you didn't get to see how everything turned out.

To my family: Matt, Rachel, Sam, Meg, and Abigail. Thank you for loving me and listening to me talk about my book, even after you'd heard about it a hundred (okay, a thousand) times before. To my mom and dad, who are always down to let me process a scene out loud in the middle of the day, and to my large extended family: I love you all.

And especially to my husband, Jim: You're the reason I am able to do what I do. I'd marry you again in a heartbeat.

One last note: Sometimes I like to use real people's names in my books. But it should be noted that while some of the names are real, the characters are purely fictional. In addition, I like to use real places. For instance, Felix's school, Orange Middle School, actually exists. It does not, however, have a Forensic Science Club. But it totally should. Just saying.